STONE ARCH BOOKS
a capstone imprint

STONE ARCH BOOKS™

Published in 2014
A Capstone Imprint
1710 Roe Crest Drive
North Mankato, MN 56003
www.capstonepub.com

Originally published by DC Comics in the U.S. in single magazine form as Teen Titans GO! #2.


DC Comics
1700 Broadway, New York, NY 10019
A Warner Bros. Entertainment Company



Cataloging-in-Publication Data is available at the Library of Congress website:
ISBN: 978-1-4342-6433-6 (library binding)

Summary: Having a sense of humor isn't always such a good thing... at least that's what Beast Boy's teammates think, since they tend to be the victims of his jokes.

STONE ARCH BOOKS
Ashley C. Andersen Zantop *Publisher*
Michael Dahl *Editorial Director*
Sean Tulien *Editor*
Heather Kindseth *Creative Director*
Alison Thiele *Designer*
Kathy McColley *Production Specialist*

DC COMICS
Kristy Quinn Original U.S. Editor

Printed and bound in the USA.
102016 010131R

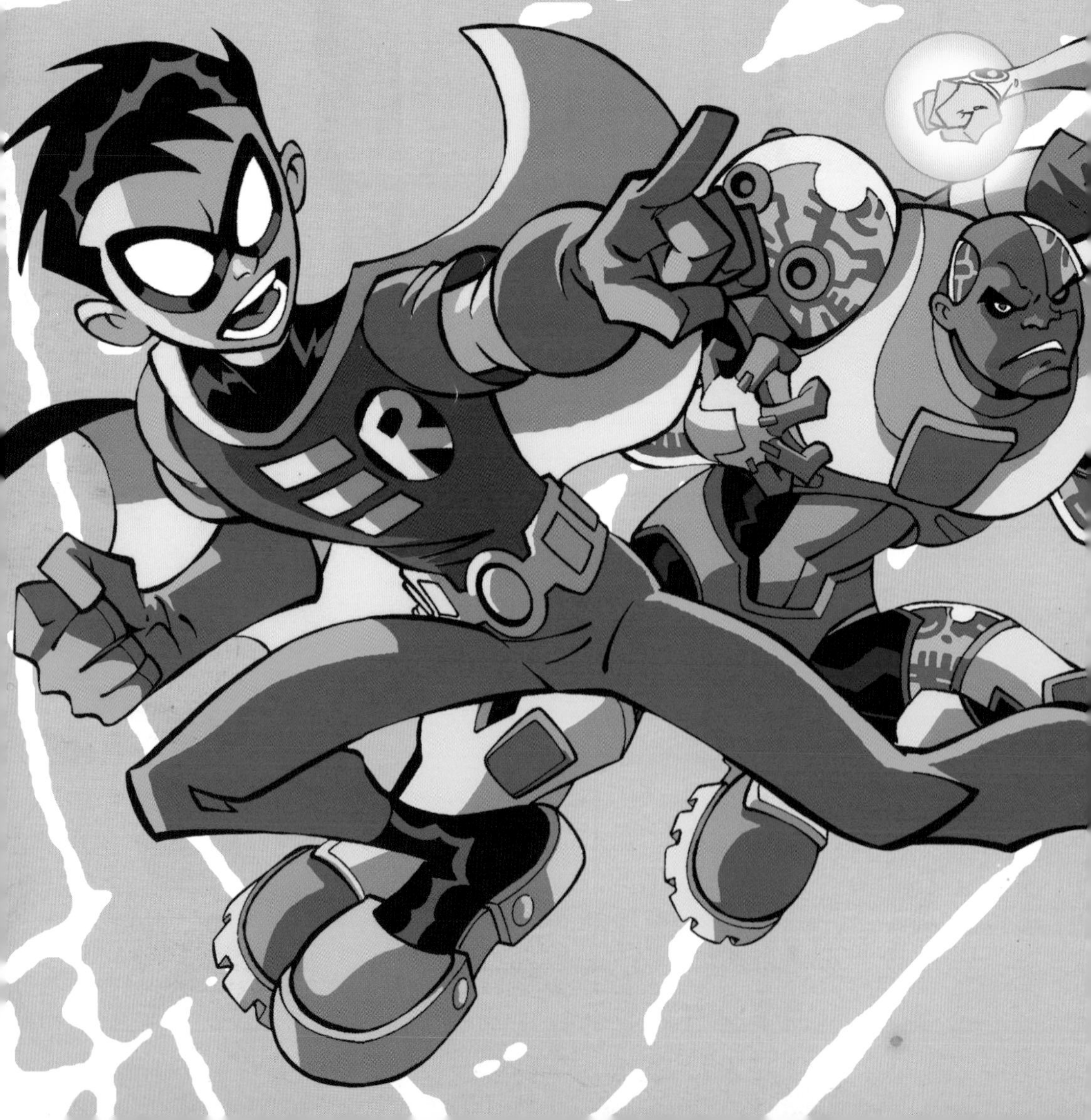

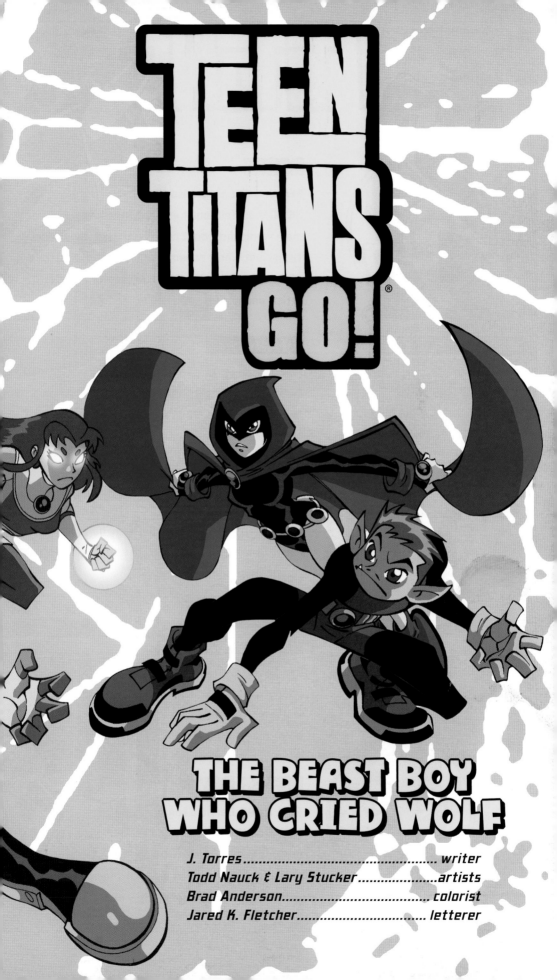

# TEEN TITANS GO!

## THE BEAST BOY WHO CRIED WOLF

J. Torres...................................................... writer
Todd Nauck & Lary Stucker.......................artists
Brad Anderson........................................... colorist
Jared K. Fletcher.................................... letterer

# TEEN TITANS GO!

### ROBIN

**REAL NAME:** Dick Grayson

**BIO:** The perfectionist leader of the group has one main complaint about his teammates: the other Titans just won't do what he says. As the partner of Batman, Robin is a talented acrobat, martial artist, and hacker.

### STARFIRE

**REAL NAME:** Princess Koriand'r

**BIO:** Formerly a warrior Princess of the now-destroyed planet Tamaran, Starfire found a new home on Earth, and a new family in the Teen Titans.

### CYBORG

**REAL NAME:** Victor Stone

**BIO:** Cyborg is a laid-back half teen, half robot who's more interested in eating pizza and playing video games than fighting crime.

### RAVEN

**REAL NAME:** Raven

**BIO:** Raven is an Azarathian empath who can teleport and control her "soul-self," which can fight physically as well as act as Raven's eyes and ears away from her body.

### BEAST BOY

**REAL NAME:** Garfield Logan

**BIO:** Beast Boy is Cyborg's best bud. He's a slightly dim but lovable loafer who can transform into all sorts of animals (when he's not too busy eating burritos and watching TV). He's also a vegetarian.

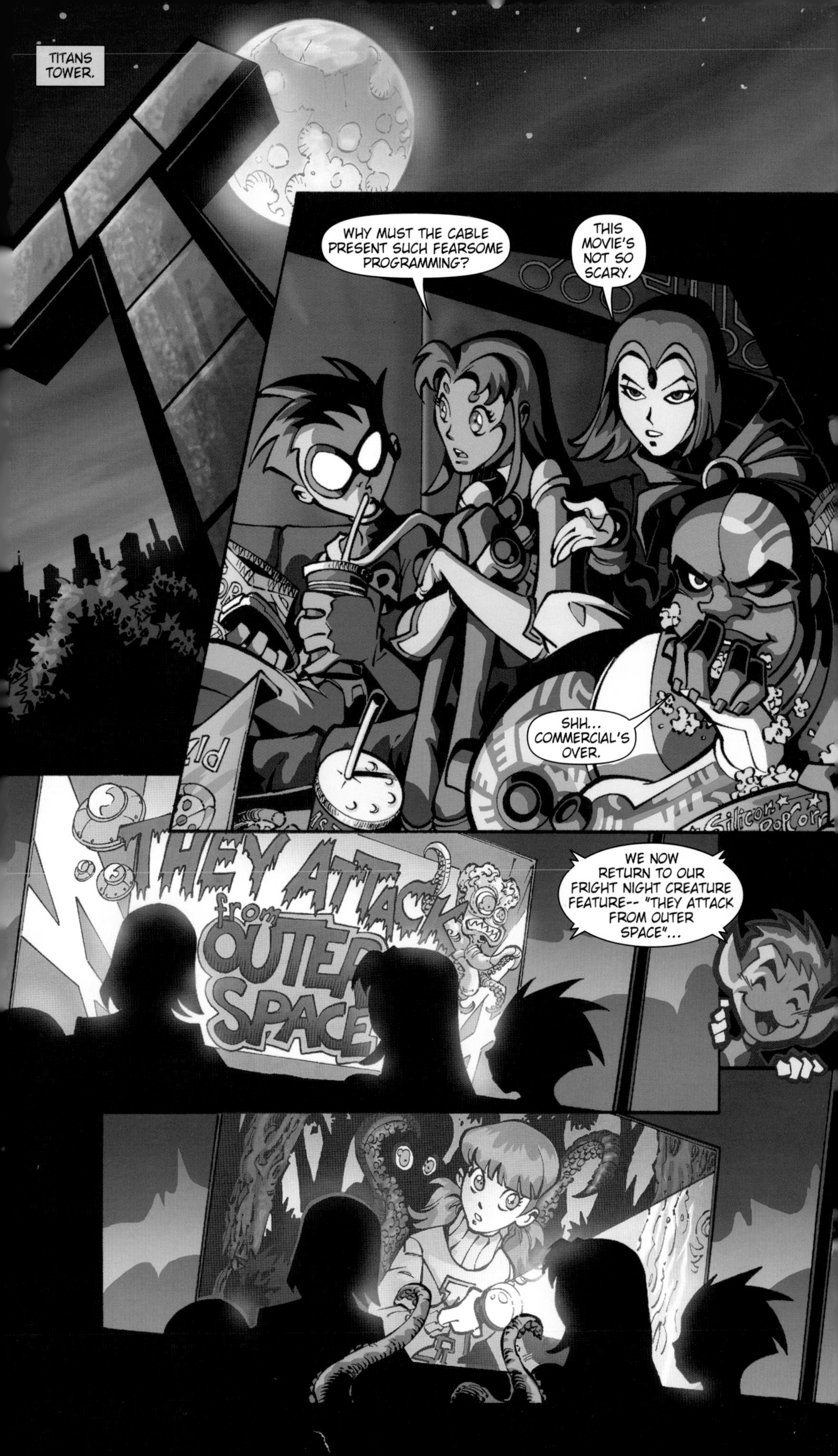
TITANS TOWER.
WHY MUST THE CABLE PRESENT SUCH FEARSOME PROGRAMMING?
THIS MOVIE'S NOT SO SCARY.
SHH... COMMERCIAL'S OVER.
Silicon PopCorn
THEY ATTACK from OUTER SPACE
WE NOW RETURN TO OUR FRIGHT NIGHT CREATURE FEATURE-- "THEY ATTACK FROM OUTER SPACE"...

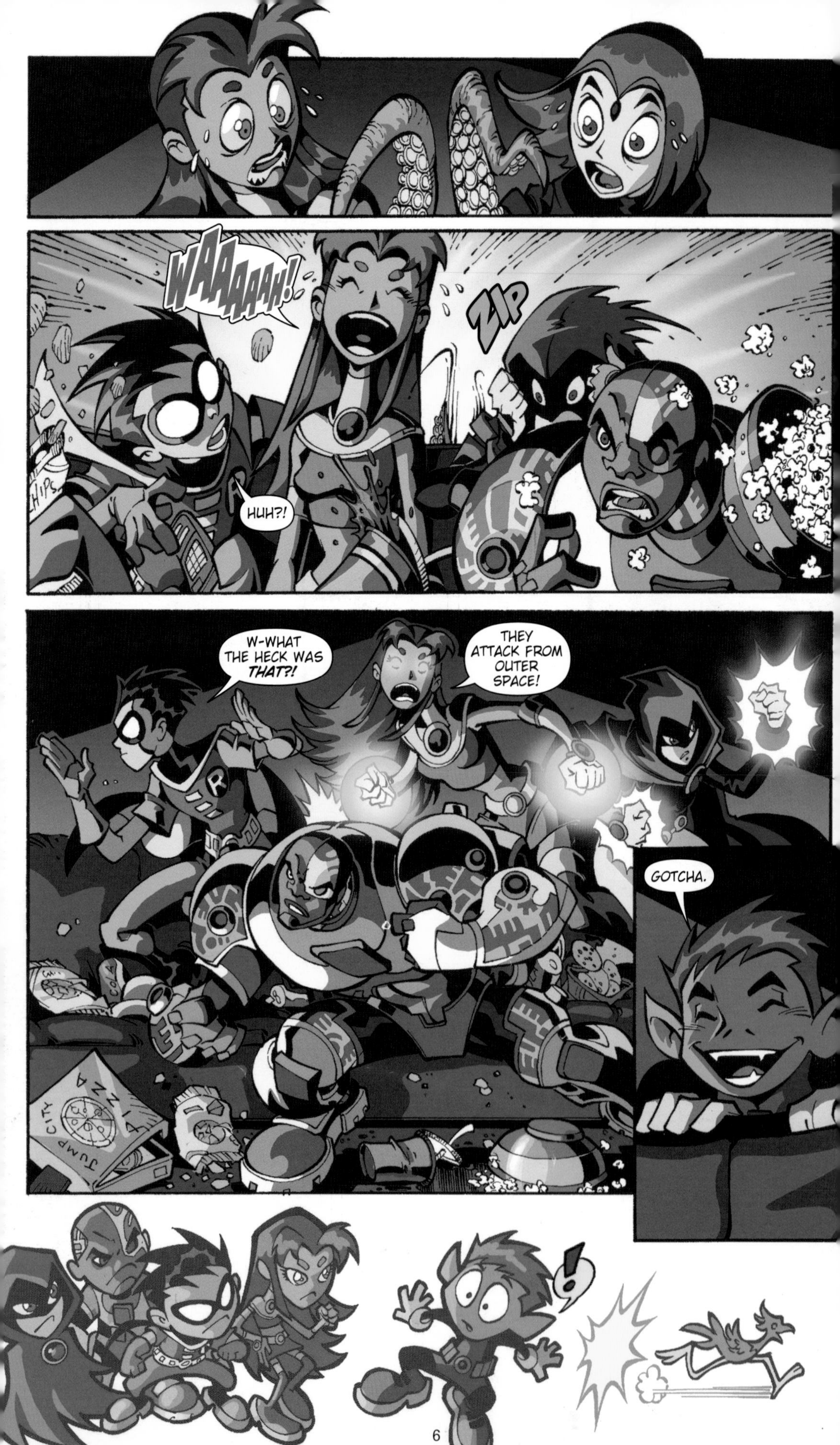
WAAAAAH!
ZIP
HUH?!
CHIPS
W-WHAT THE HECK WAS *THAT?!*
THEY ATTACK FROM OUTER SPACE!
GOTCHA.
JUMP CITY PIZZA
!

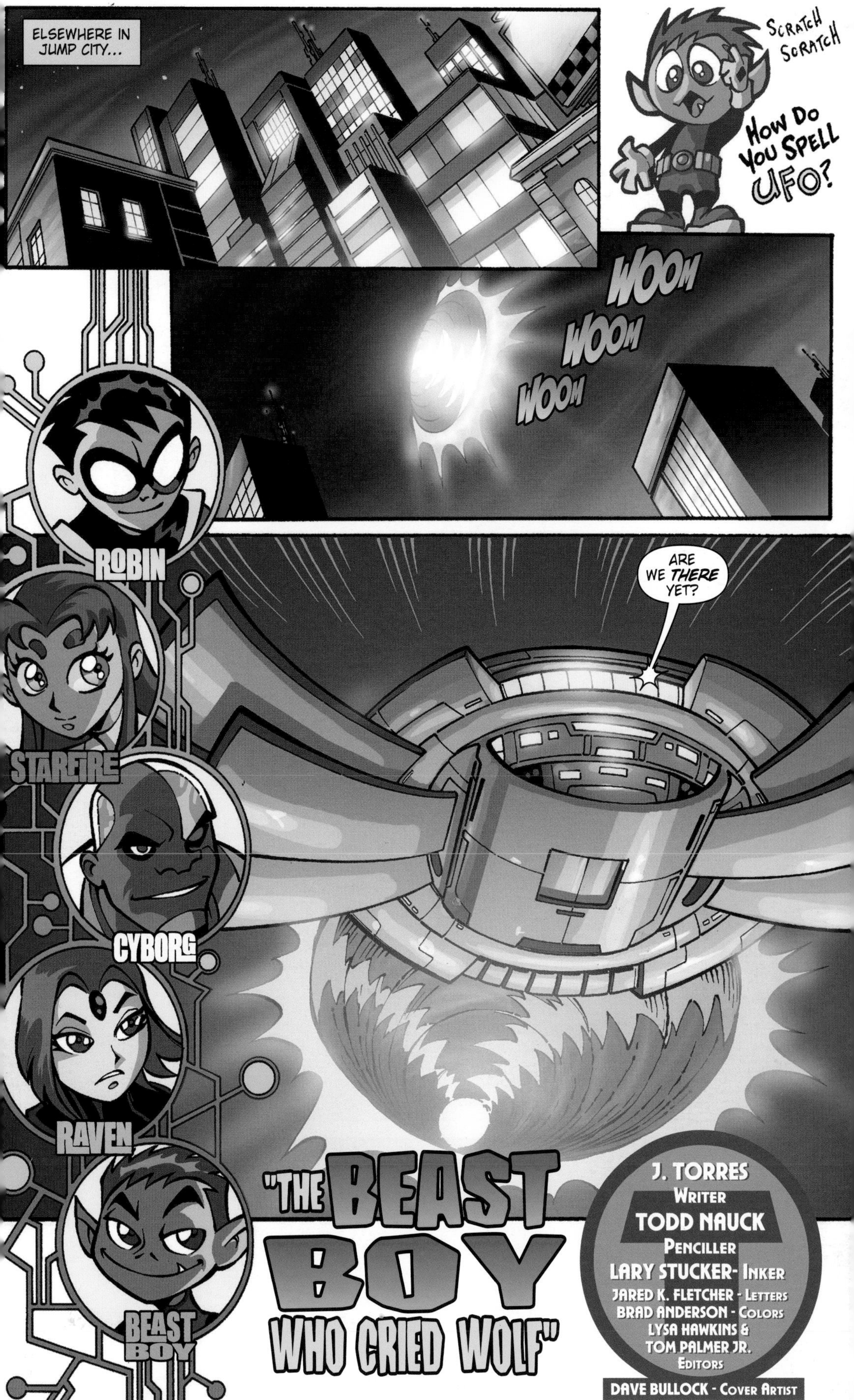
ELSEWHERE IN JUMP CITY...
SCRATCH SCRATCH
HOW DO YOU SPELL UFO?
WOOM
WOOM
WOOM
ROBIN
ARE WE THERE YET?
STARFIRE
CYBORG
RAVEN
BEAST BOY
"THE BEAST BOY WHO CRIED WOLF"
J. TORRES Writer
TODD NAUCK Penciller
LARY STUCKER- Inker
JARED K. FLETCHER - Letters
BRAD ANDERSON - Colors
LYSA HAWKINS & TOM PALMER JR. Editors
DAVE BULLOCK - Cover Artist

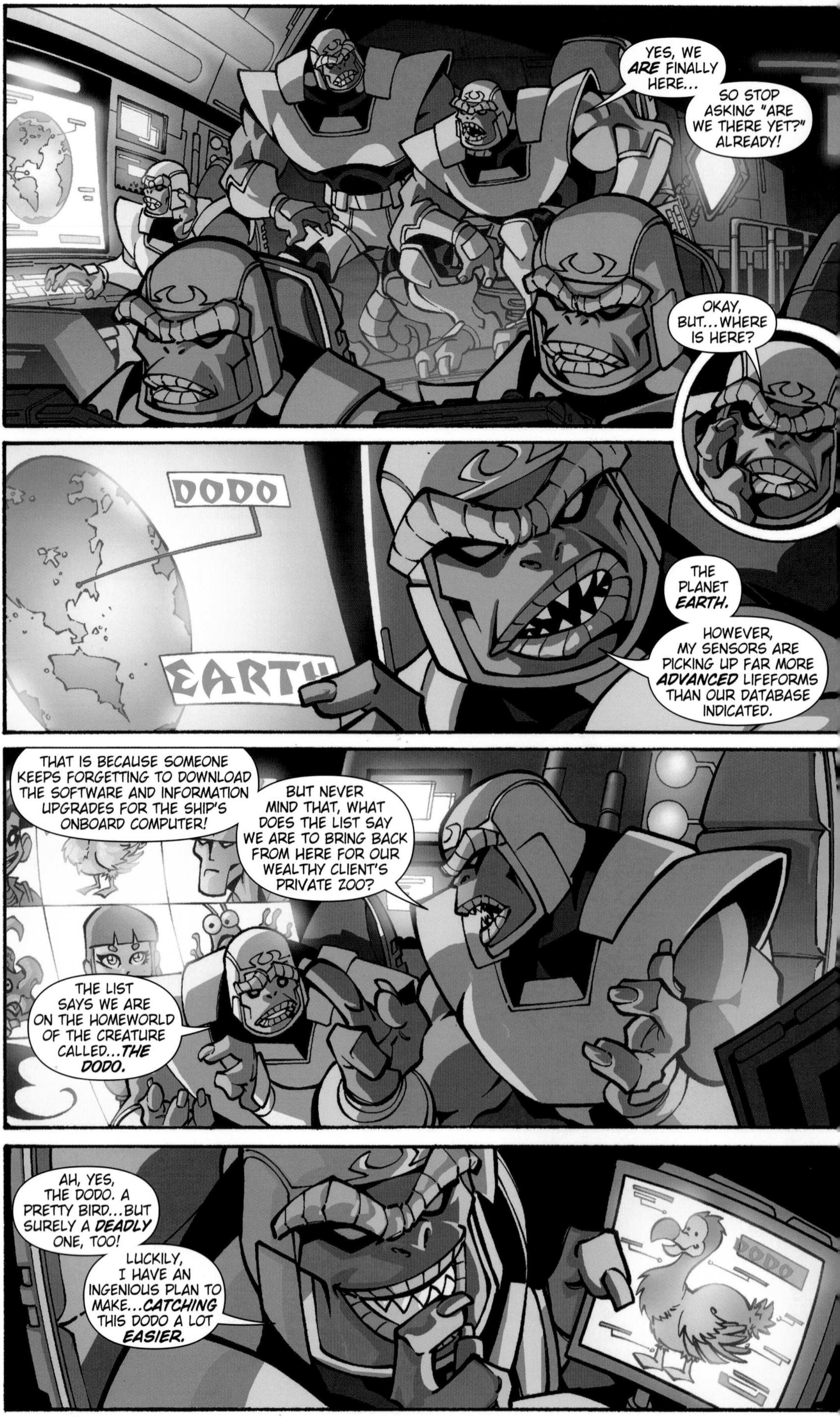
YES, WE ARE FINALLY HERE...
SO STOP ASKING "ARE WE THERE YET?" ALREADY!
OKAY, BUT...WHERE IS HERE?
DODO
EARTH
THE PLANET EARTH.
HOWEVER, MY SENSORS ARE PICKING UP FAR MORE ADVANCED LIFEFORMS THAN OUR DATABASE INDICATED.
THAT IS BECAUSE SOMEONE KEEPS FORGETTING TO DOWNLOAD THE SOFTWARE AND INFORMATION UPGRADES FOR THE SHIP'S ONBOARD COMPUTER!
BUT NEVER MIND THAT, WHAT DOES THE LIST SAY WE ARE TO BRING BACK FROM HERE FOR OUR WEALTHY CLIENT'S PRIVATE ZOO?
THE LIST SAYS WE ARE ON THE HOMEWORLD OF THE CREATURE CALLED...THE DODO.
AH, YES, THE DODO. A PRETTY BIRD...BUT SURELY A DEADLY ONE, TOO!
LUCKILY, I HAVE AN INGENIOUS PLAN TO MAKE...CATCHING THIS DODO A LOT EASIER.
DODO

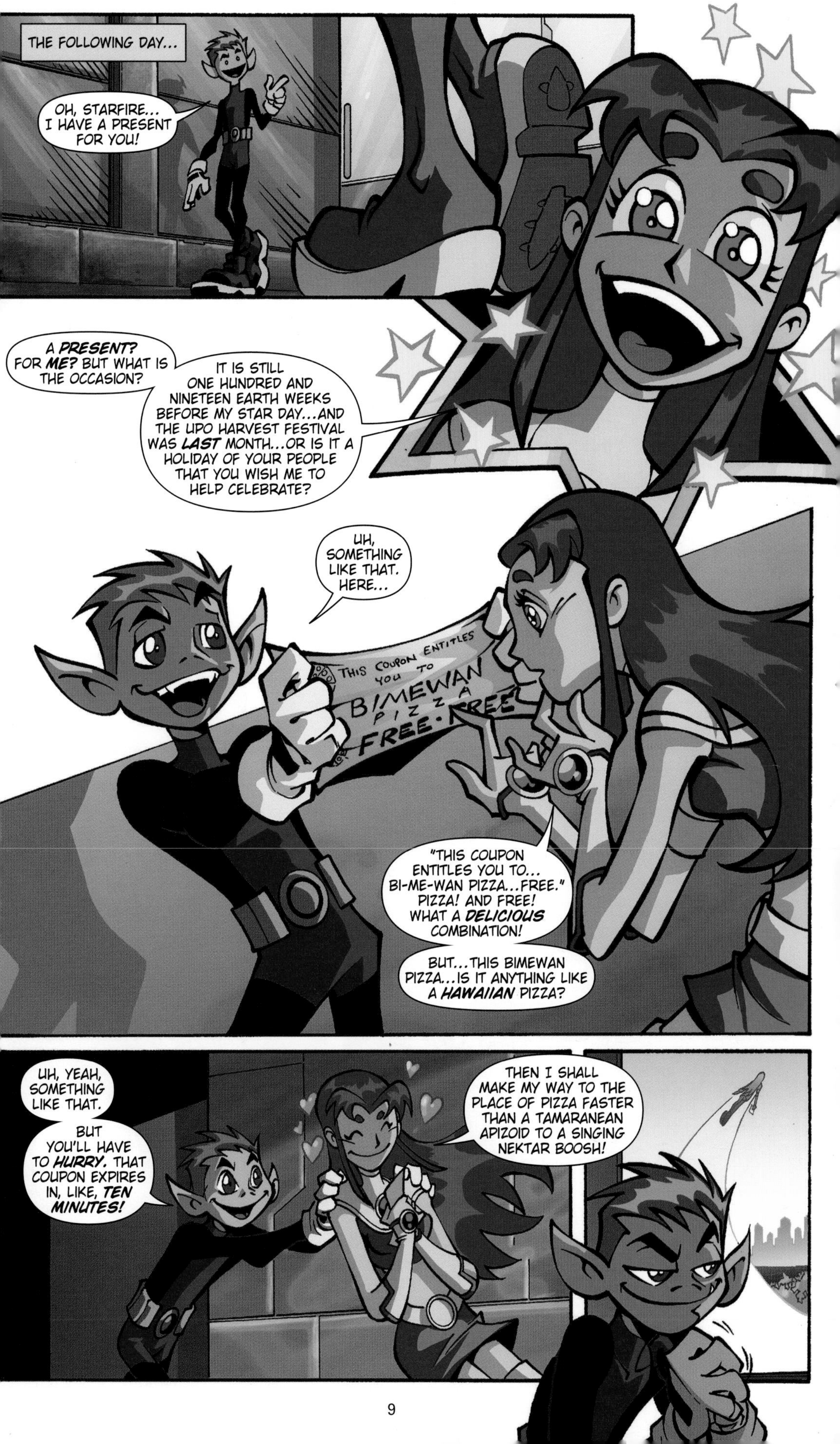
THE FOLLOWING DAY...
OH, STARFIRE... I HAVE A PRESENT FOR YOU!
A PRESENT? FOR ME? BUT WHAT IS THE OCCASION?
IT IS STILL ONE HUNDRED AND NINETEEN EARTH WEEKS BEFORE MY STAR DAY...AND THE UPO HARVEST FESTIVAL WAS LAST MONTH...OR IS IT A HOLIDAY OF YOUR PEOPLE THAT YOU WISH ME TO HELP CELEBRATE?
UH, SOMETHING LIKE THAT. HERE...
THIS COUPON ENTITLES YOU TO BIMEWAN PIZZA FREE
"THIS COUPON ENTITLES YOU TO... BI-ME-WAN PIZZA...FREE." PIZZA! AND FREE! WHAT A DELICIOUS COMBINATION!
BUT...THIS BIMEWAN PIZZA...IS IT ANYTHING LIKE A HAWAIIAN PIZZA?
UH, YEAH, SOMETHING LIKE THAT.
BUT YOU'LL HAVE TO HURRY. THAT COUPON EXPIRES IN, LIKE, TEN MINUTES!
THEN I SHALL MAKE MY WAY TO THE PLACE OF PIZZA FASTER THAN A TAMARANEAN APIZOID TO A SINGING NEKTAR BOOSH!

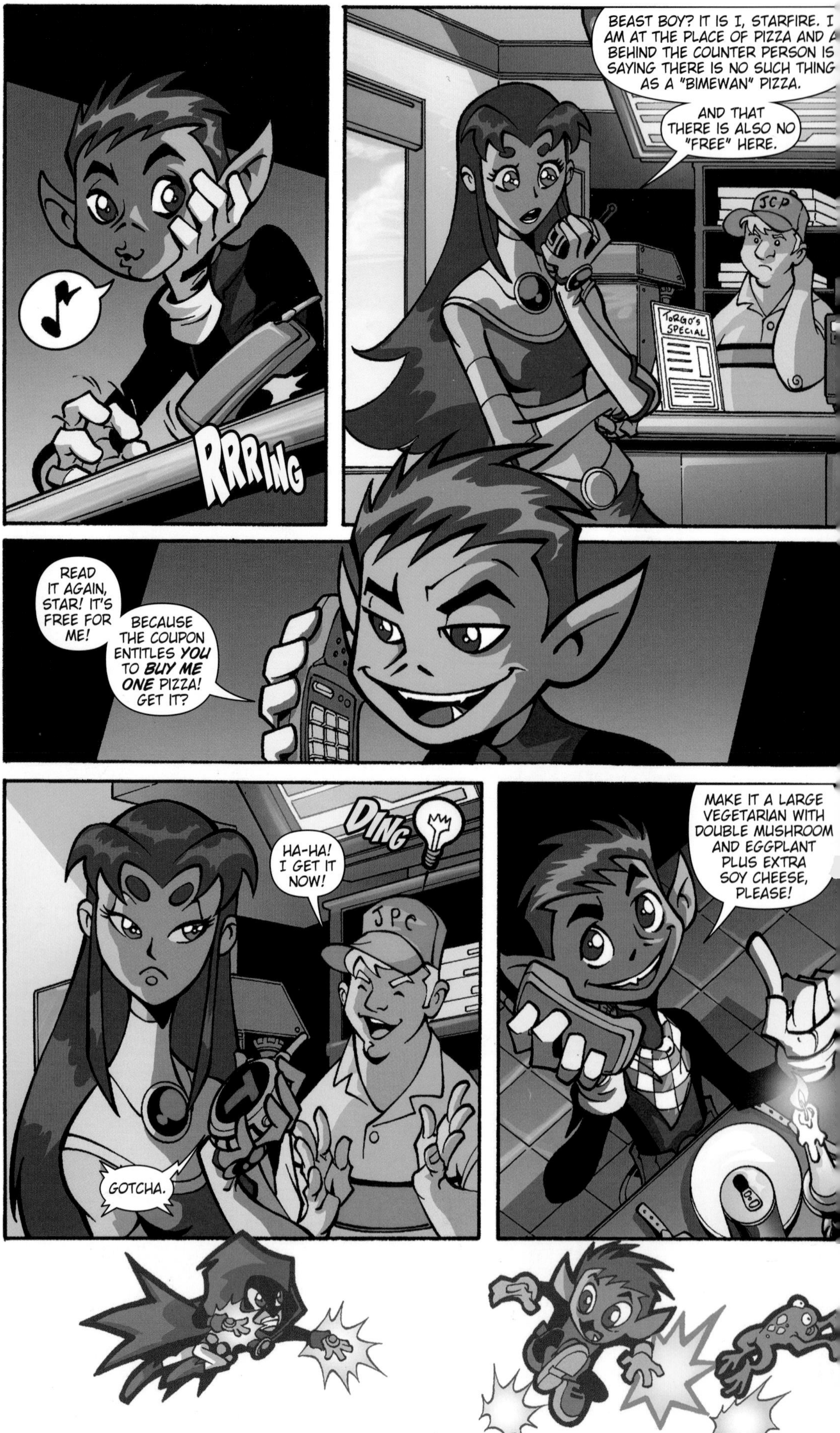

RRRING
BEAST BOY? IT IS I, STARFIRE. I AM AT THE PLACE OF PIZZA AND A BEHIND THE COUNTER PERSON IS SAYING THERE IS NO SUCH THING AS A "BIMEWAN" PIZZA.
AND THAT THERE IS ALSO NO "FREE" HERE.
JCP
TORGO'S SPECIAL
READ IT AGAIN, STAR! IT'S FREE FOR ME!
BECAUSE THE COUPON ENTITLES *YOU* TO *BUY ME ONE* PIZZA! GET IT?
DING
HA-HA! I GET IT NOW!
JPC
GOTCHA.
MAKE IT A LARGE VEGETARIAN WITH DOUBLE MUSHROOM AND EGGPLANT PLUS EXTRA SOY CHEESE, PLEASE!

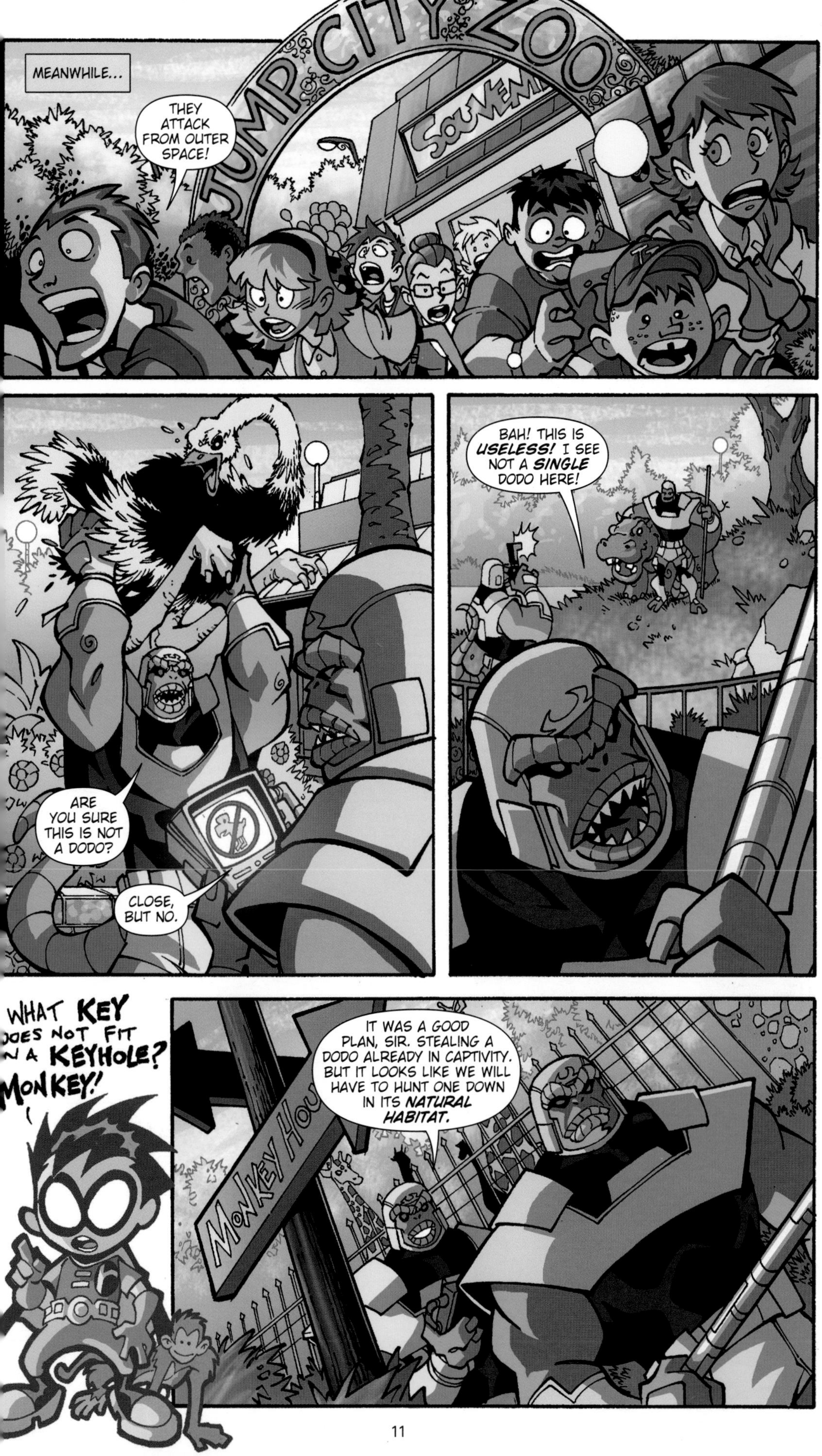
MEANWHILE...
JUMP CITY ZOO
THEY ATTACK FROM OUTER SPACE!
ARE YOU SURE THIS IS NOT A DODO?
CLOSE, BUT NO.
BAH! THIS IS **USELESS!** I SEE NOT A **SINGLE** DODO HERE!
IT WAS A GOOD PLAN, SIR. STEALING A DODO ALREADY IN CAPTIVITY. BUT IT LOOKS LIKE WE WILL HAVE TO HUNT ONE DOWN IN ITS **NATURAL HABITAT.**
WHAT KEY
OES NOT FIT
N A KEYHOLE?
MONKEY!

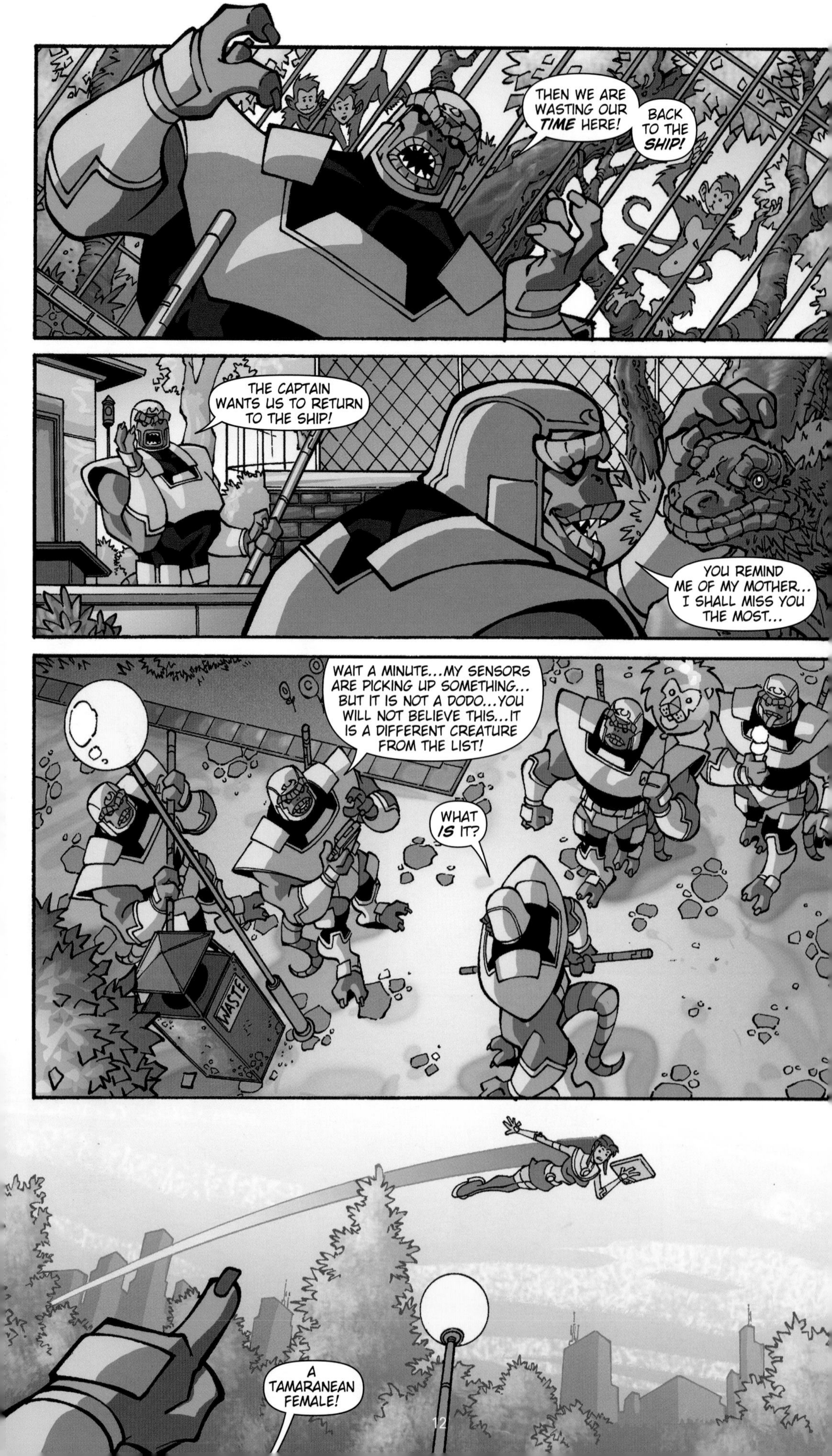
THEN WE ARE WASTING OUR TIME HERE!
BACK TO THE SHIP!
THE CAPTAIN WANTS US TO RETURN TO THE SHIP!
YOU REMIND ME OF MY MOTHER... I SHALL MISS YOU THE MOST...
WAIT A MINUTE...MY SENSORS ARE PICKING UP SOMETHING... BUT IT IS NOT A DODO...YOU WILL NOT BELIEVE THIS...IT IS A DIFFERENT CREATURE FROM THE LIST!
WHAT IS IT?
WASTE
A TAMARANEAN FEMALE!

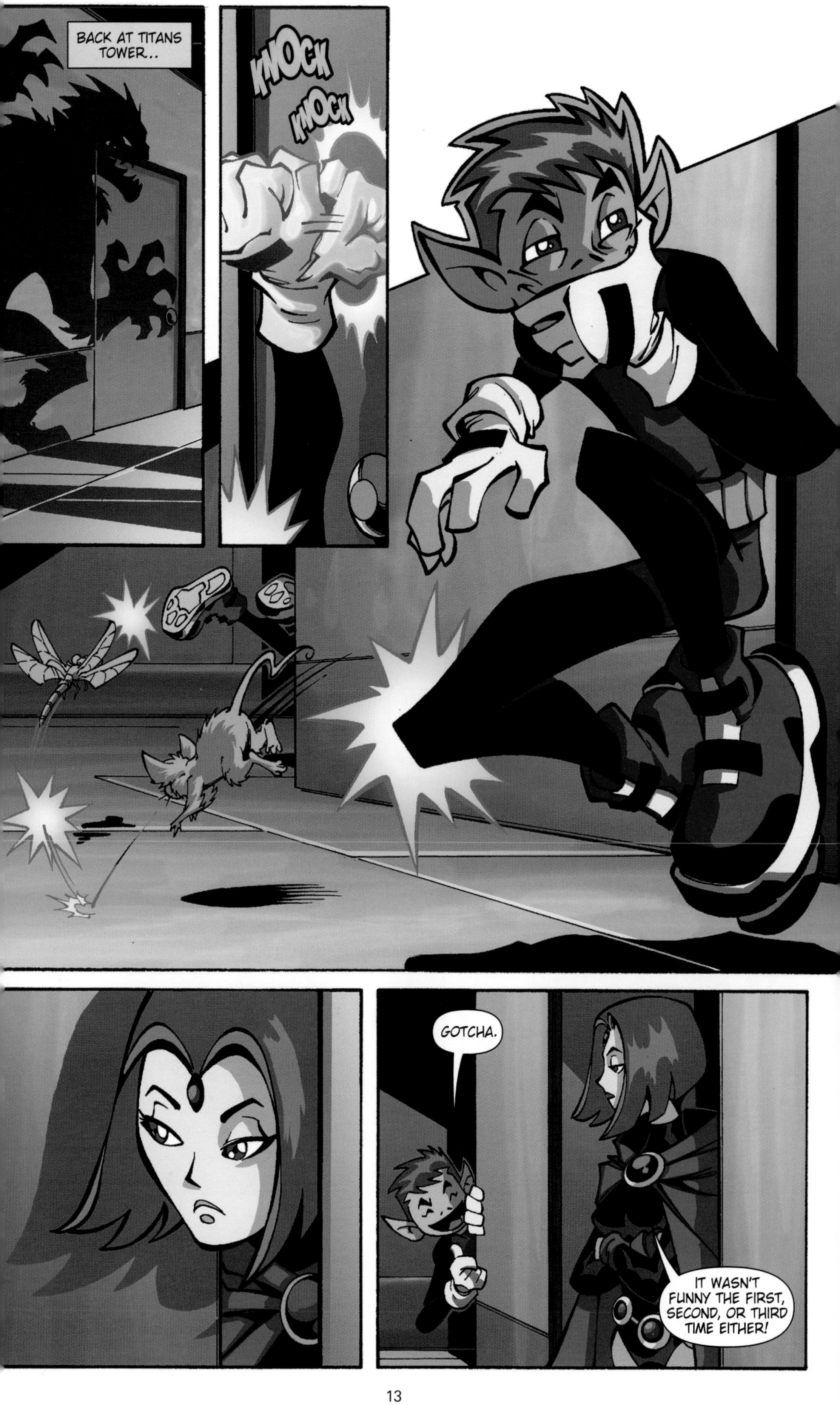
BACK AT TITANS TOWER...
KNOCK
KNOCK
GOTCHA.
IT WASN'T FUNNY THE FIRST, SECOND, OR THIRD TIME EITHER!

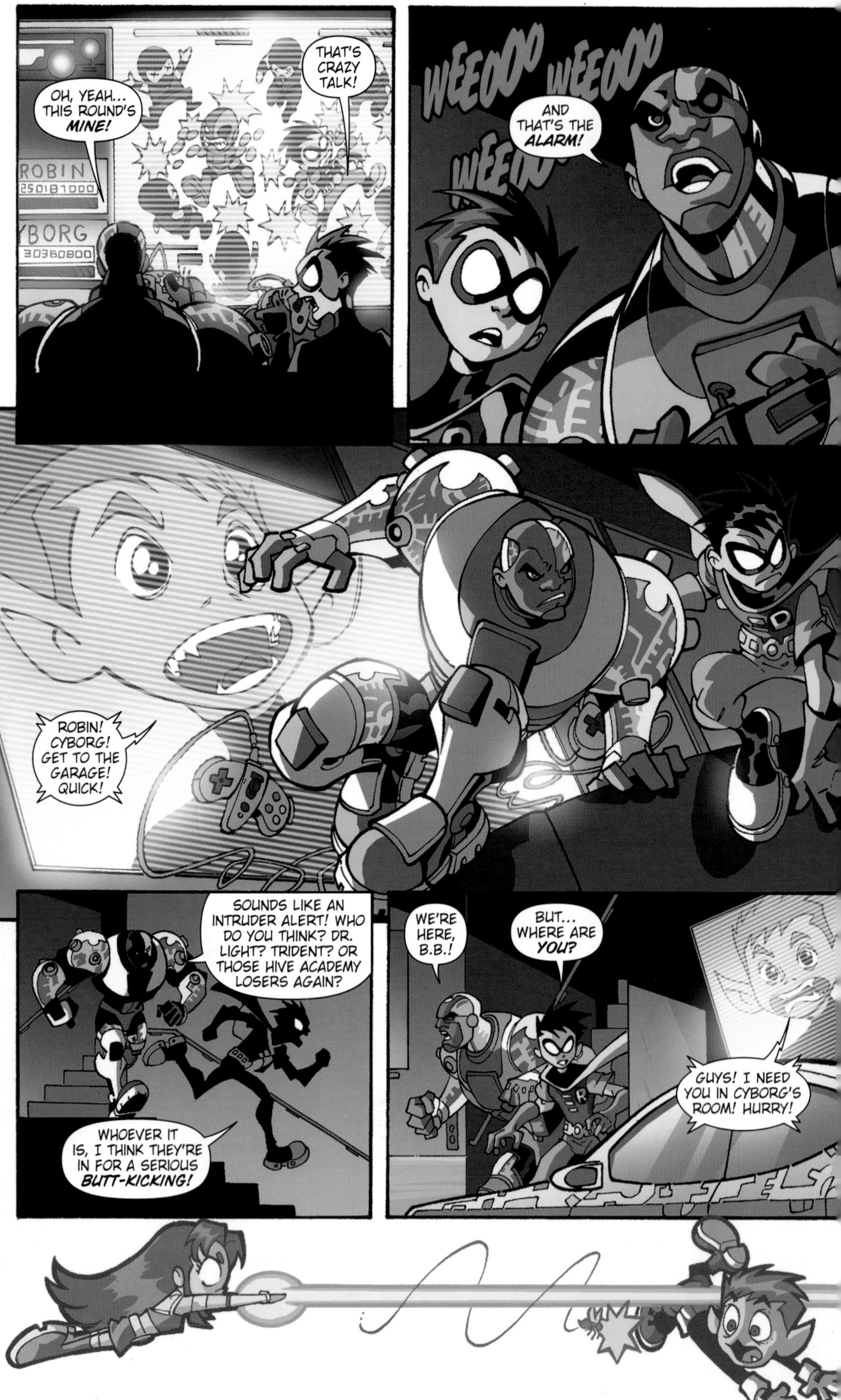
OH, YEAH... THIS ROUND'S MINE!
THAT'S CRAZY TALK!
ROBIN
250181000
YBORG
30360800
WEEOOO WEEOOO
AND THAT'S THE ALARM!
ROBIN! CYBORG! GET TO THE GARAGE! QUICK!
SOUNDS LIKE AN INTRUDER ALERT! WHO DO YOU THINK? DR. LIGHT? TRIDENT? OR THOSE HIVE ACADEMY LOSERS AGAIN?
WHOEVER IT IS, I THINK THEY'RE IN FOR A SERIOUS BUTT-KICKING!
WE'RE HERE, B.B.!
BUT... WHERE ARE YOU?
GUYS! I NEED YOU IN CYBORG'S ROOM! HURRY!

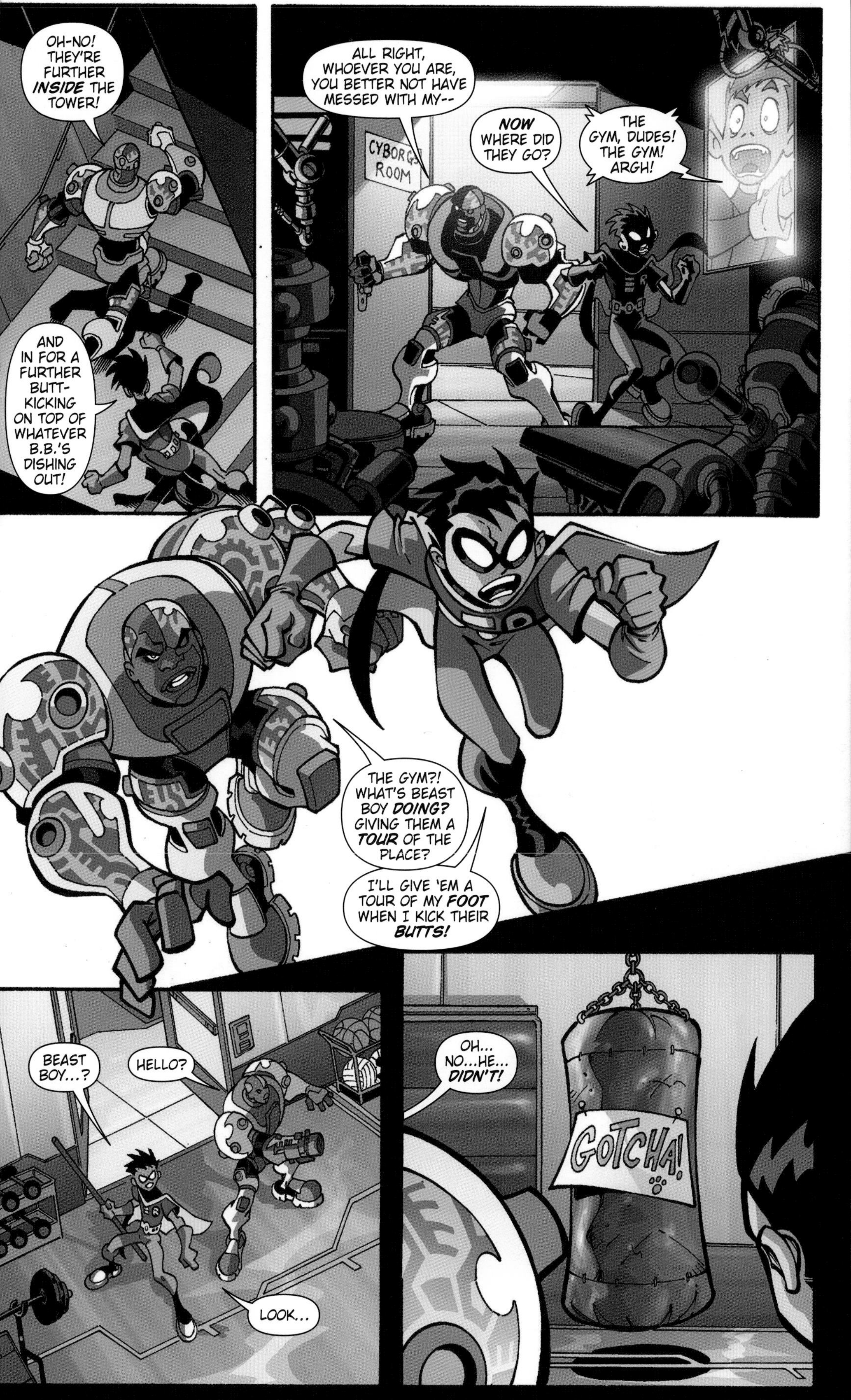
OH-NO! THEY'RE FURTHER INSIDE THE TOWER!
AND IN FOR A FURTHER BUTT-KICKING ON TOP OF WHATEVER B.B.'S DISHING OUT!
ALL RIGHT, WHOEVER YOU ARE, YOU BETTER NOT HAVE MESSED WITH MY--
CYBORG'S ROOM
NOW WHERE DID THEY GO?
THE GYM, DUDES! THE GYM! ARGH!
THE GYM?! WHAT'S BEAST BOY DOING? GIVING THEM A TOUR OF THE PLACE?
I'LL GIVE 'EM A TOUR OF MY FOOT WHEN I KICK THEIR BUTTS!
BEAST BOY...?
HELLO?
LOOK...
OH... NO...HE... DIDN'T!
GOTCHA!

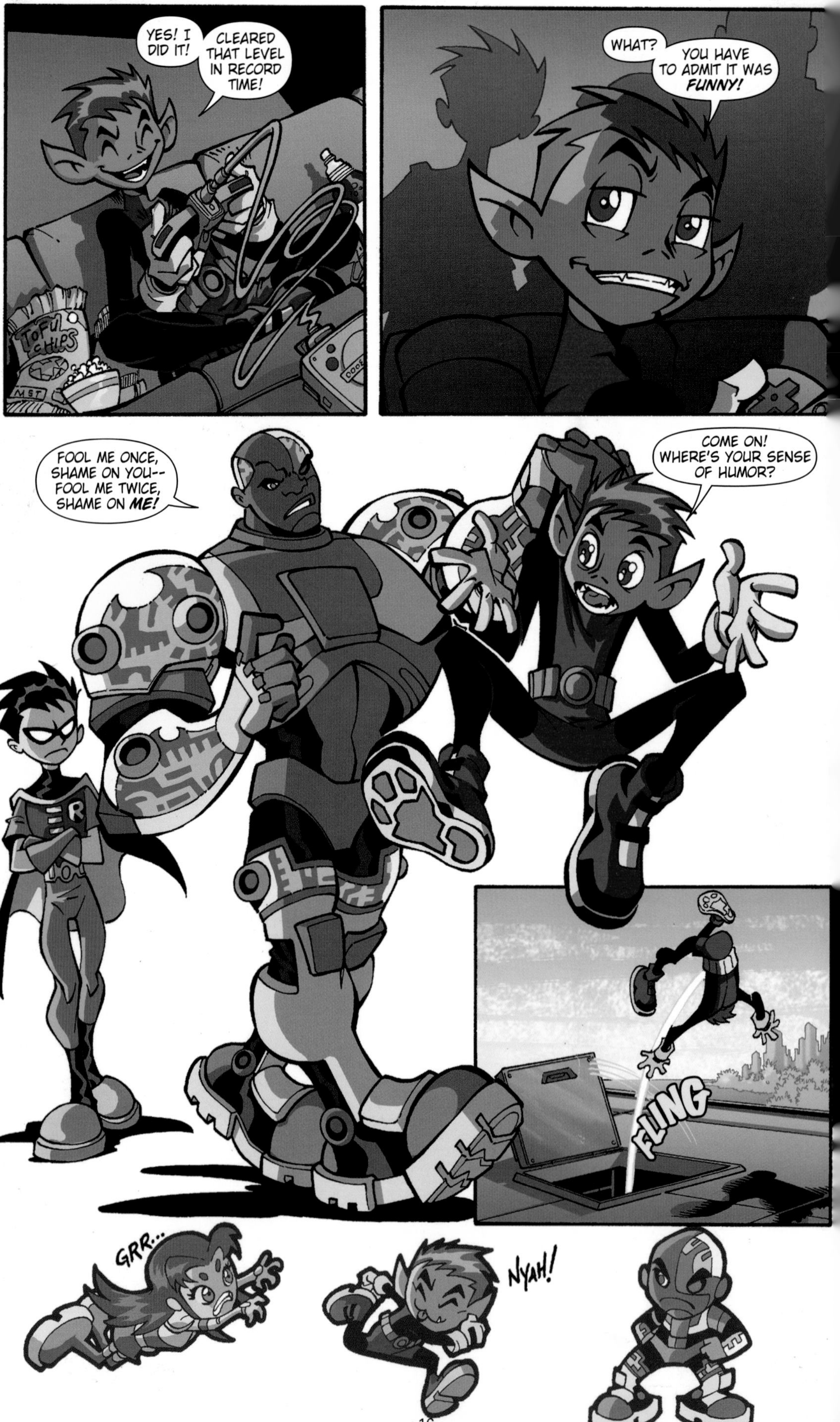
YES! I DID IT!
CLEARED THAT LEVEL IN RECORD TIME!
TOFU CHIPS
WHAT?
YOU HAVE TO ADMIT IT WAS FUNNY!
FOOL ME ONCE, SHAME ON YOU-- FOOL ME TWICE, SHAME ON ME!
COME ON! WHERE'S YOUR SENSE OF HUMOR?
FLING
GRR...
NYAH!

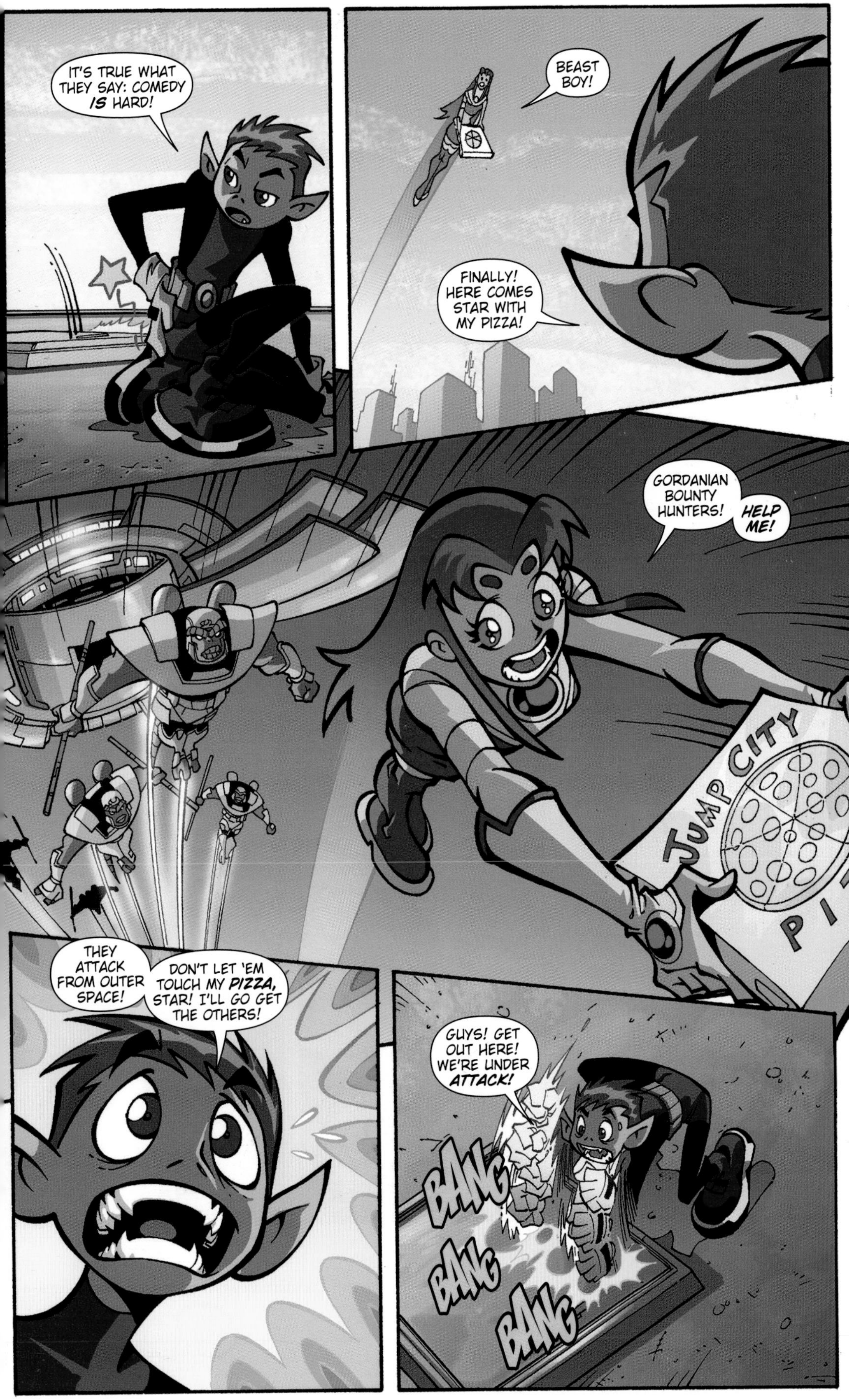
IT'S TRUE WHAT THEY SAY: COMEDY *IS* HARD!
BEAST BOY!
FINALLY! HERE COMES STAR WITH MY PIZZA!
GORDANIAN BOUNTY HUNTERS! ***HELP ME!***
JUMP CITY PI
THEY ATTACK FROM OUTER SPACE!
DON'T LET 'EM TOUCH MY ***PIZZA,*** STAR! I'LL GO GET THE OTHERS!
GUYS! GET OUT HERE! WE'RE UNDER ***ATTACK!***
BANG
BANG
BANG

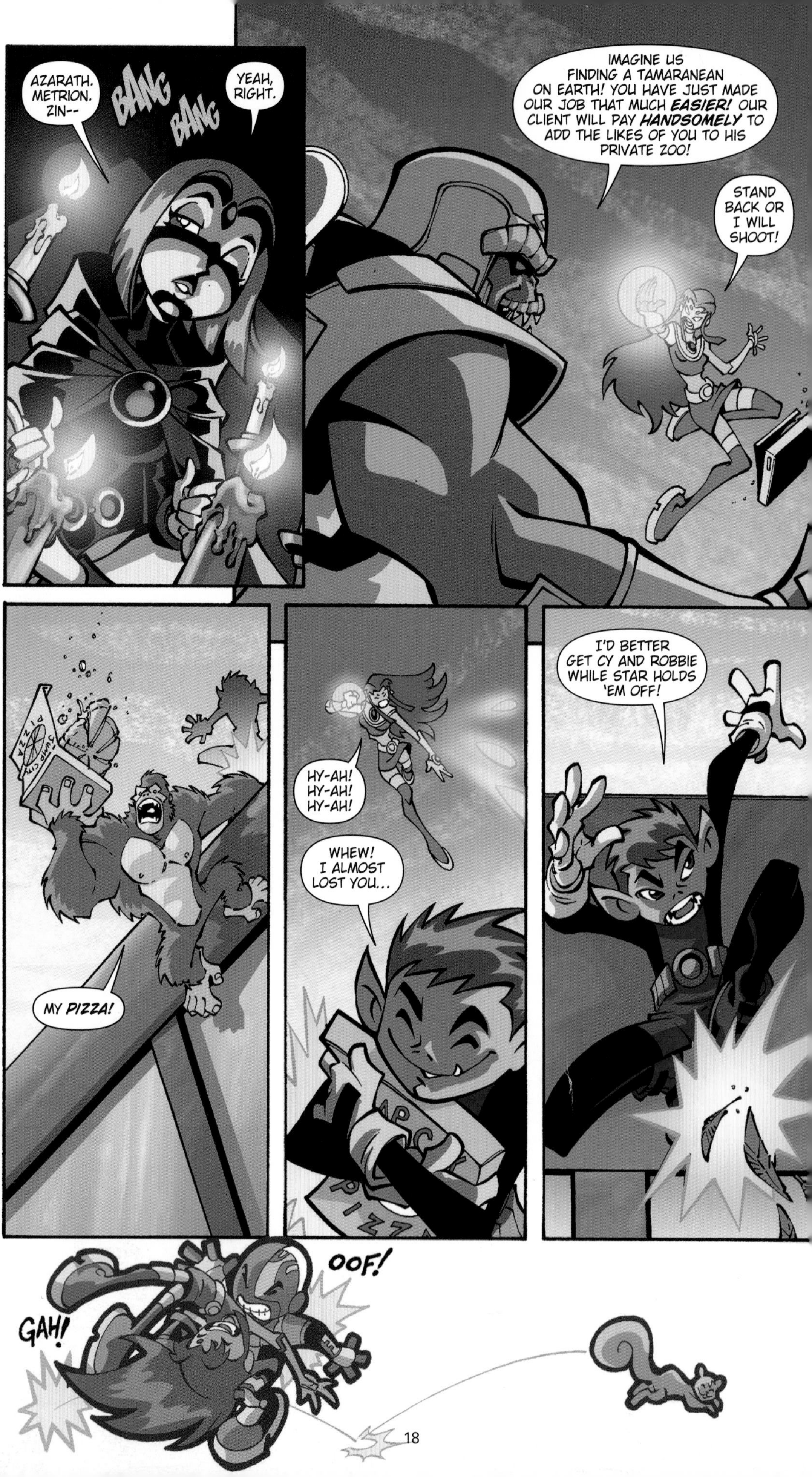
AZARATH. METRION. ZIN--
BANG BANG
YEAH, RIGHT.
IMAGINE US FINDING A TAMARANEAN ON EARTH! YOU HAVE JUST MADE OUR JOB THAT MUCH EASIER! OUR CLIENT WILL PAY HANDSOMELY TO ADD THE LIKES OF YOU TO HIS PRIVATE ZOO!
STAND BACK OR I WILL SHOOT!
MY PIZZA!
HY-AH! HY-AH! HY-AH!
WHEW! I ALMOST LOST YOU...
I'D BETTER GET CY AND ROBBIE WHILE STAR HOLDS 'EM OFF!
OOF!
GAH!

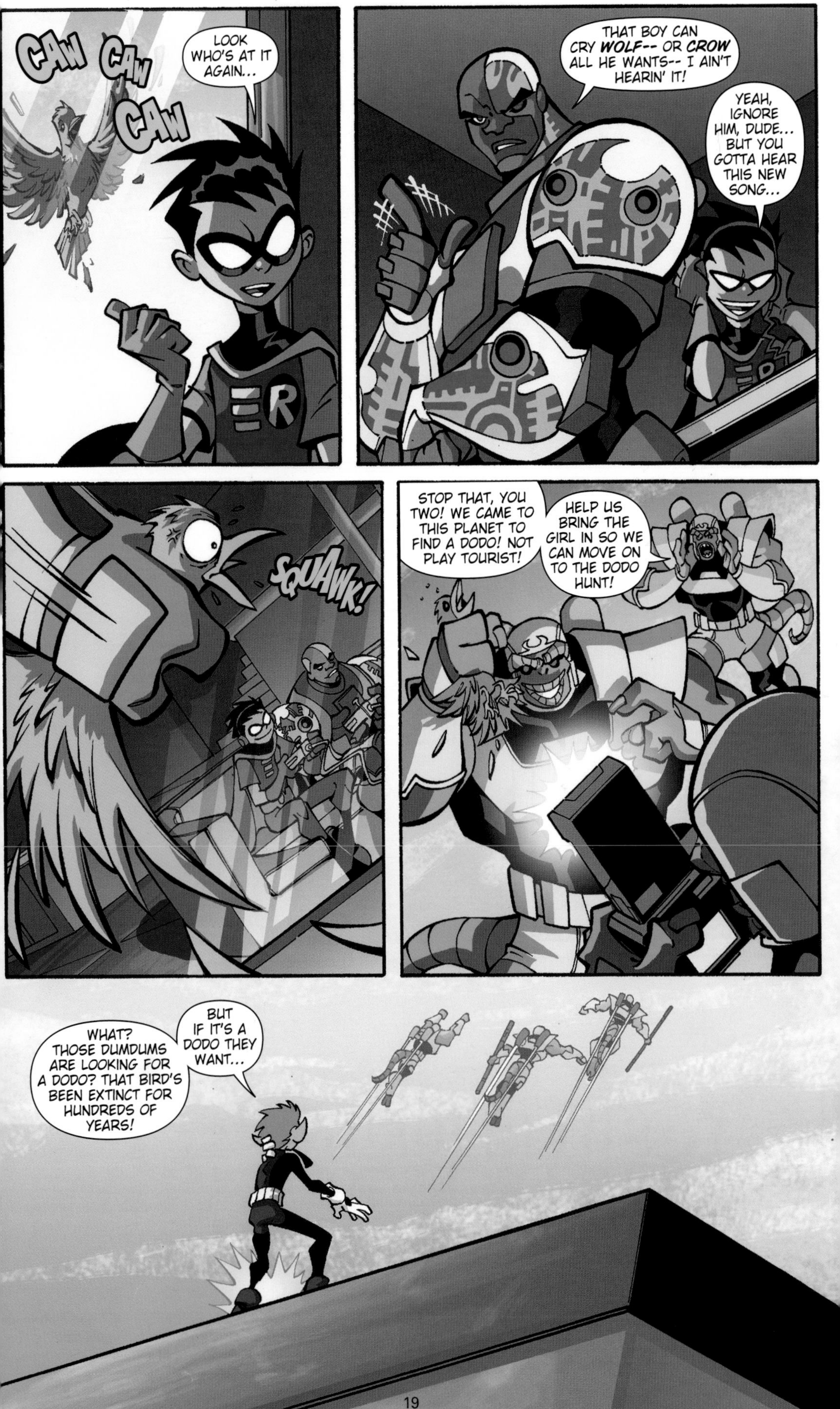
CAW CAW CAW
LOOK WHO'S AT IT AGAIN...
THAT BOY CAN CRY WOLF-- OR CROW ALL HE WANTS-- I AIN'T HEARIN' IT!
YEAH, IGNORE HIM, DUDE... BUT YOU GOTTA HEAR THIS NEW SONG...
SQUAWK!
STOP THAT, YOU TWO! WE CAME TO THIS PLANET TO FIND A DODO! NOT PLAY TOURIST!
HELP US BRING THE GIRL IN SO WE CAN MOVE ON TO THE DODO HUNT!
WHAT? THOSE DUMDUMS ARE LOOKING FOR A DODO? THAT BIRD'S BEEN EXTINCT FOR HUNDREDS OF YEARS!
BUT IF IT'S A DODO THEY WANT...

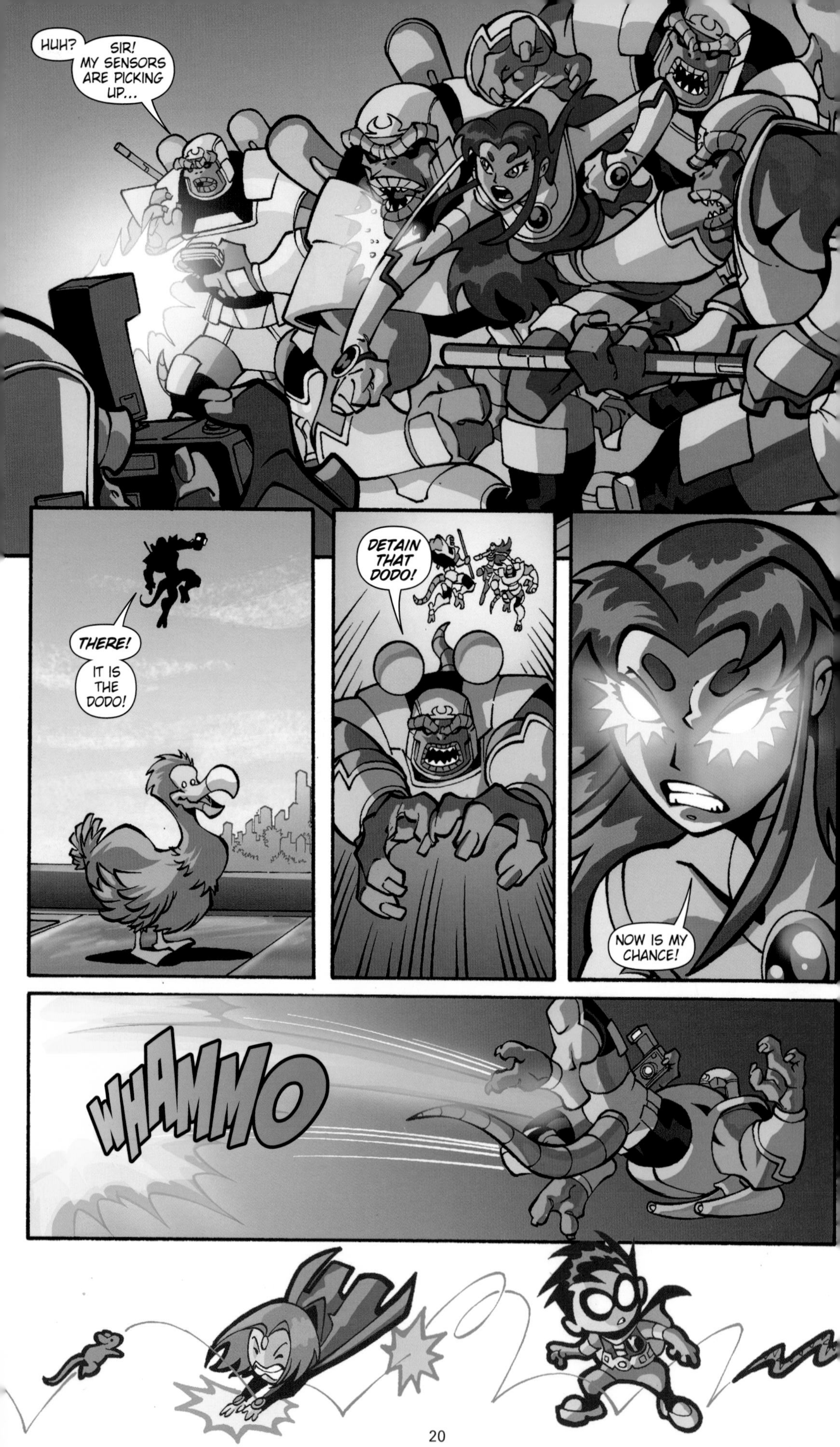
HUH?
SIR! MY SENSORS ARE PICKING UP...
THERE!
IT IS THE DODO!
DETAIN THAT DODO!
NOW IS MY CHANCE!
WHAMMO

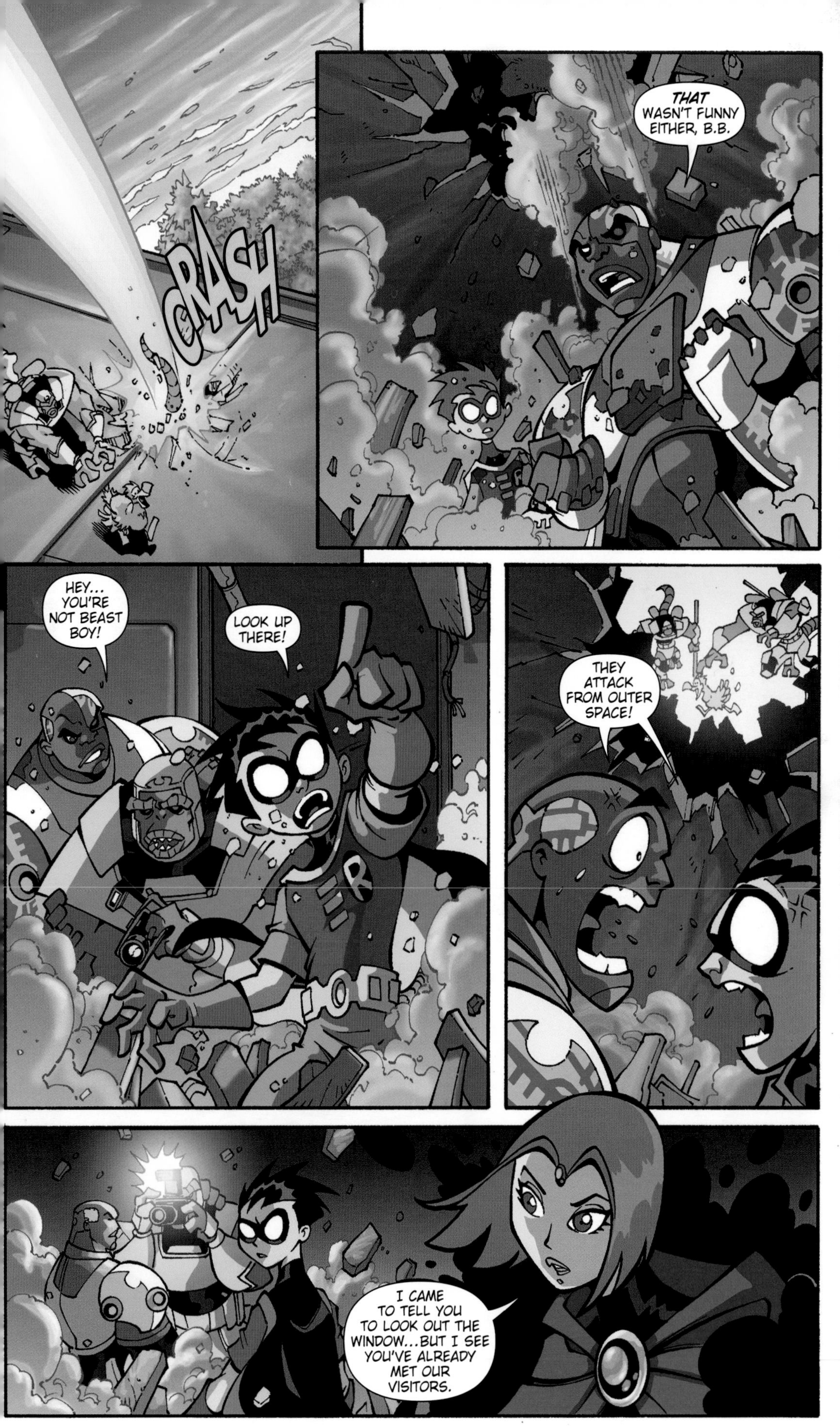
CRASH
THAT WASN'T FUNNY EITHER, B.B.
HEY... YOU'RE NOT BEAST BOY!
LOOK UP THERE!
THEY ATTACK FROM OUTER SPACE!
I CAME TO TELL YOU TO LOOK OUT THE WINDOW...BUT I SEE YOU'VE ALREADY MET OUR VISITORS.

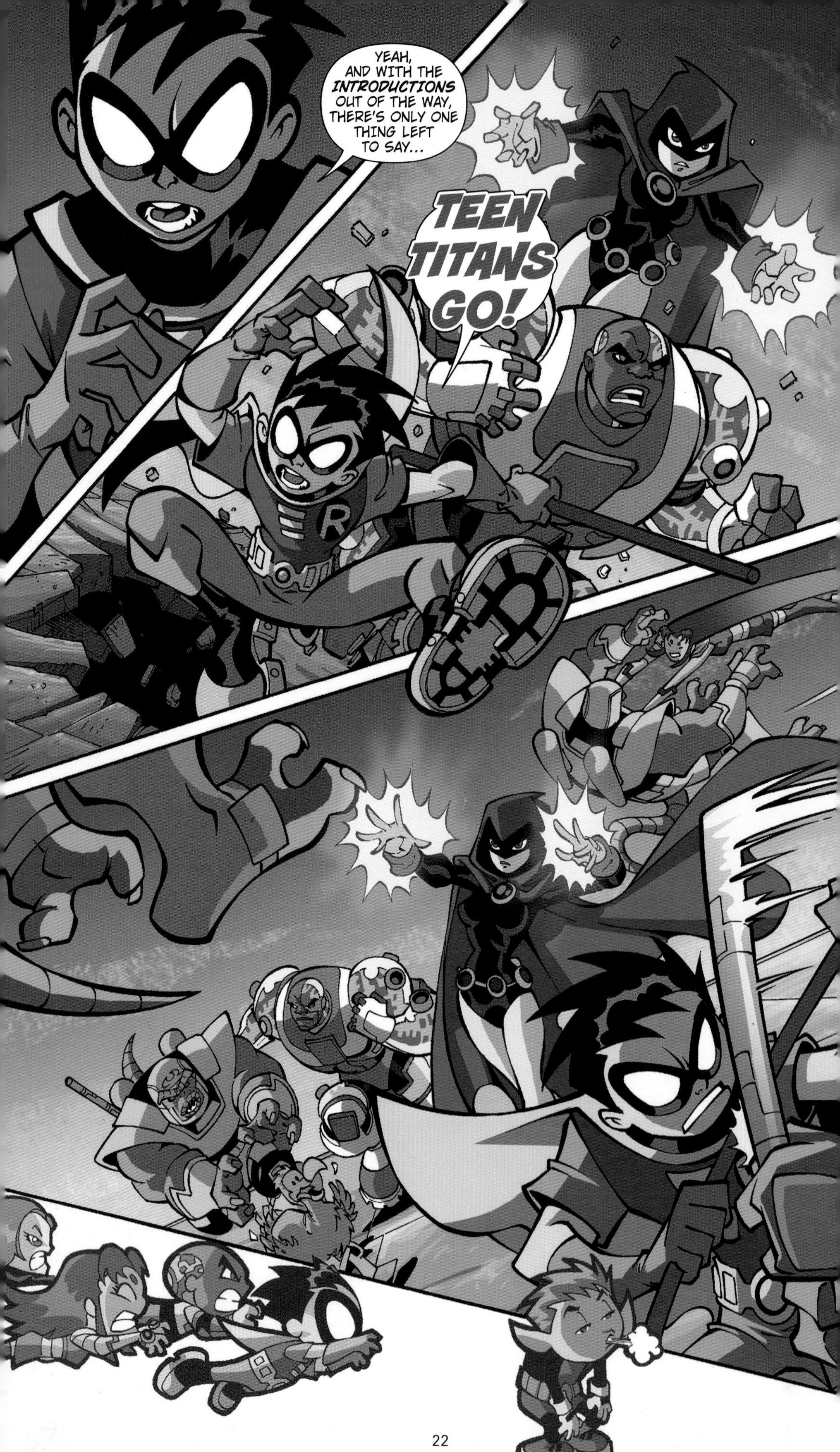
YEAH, AND WITH THE INTRODUCTIONS OUT OF THE WAY, THERE'S ONLY ONE THING LEFT TO SAY...
TEEN TITANS GO!

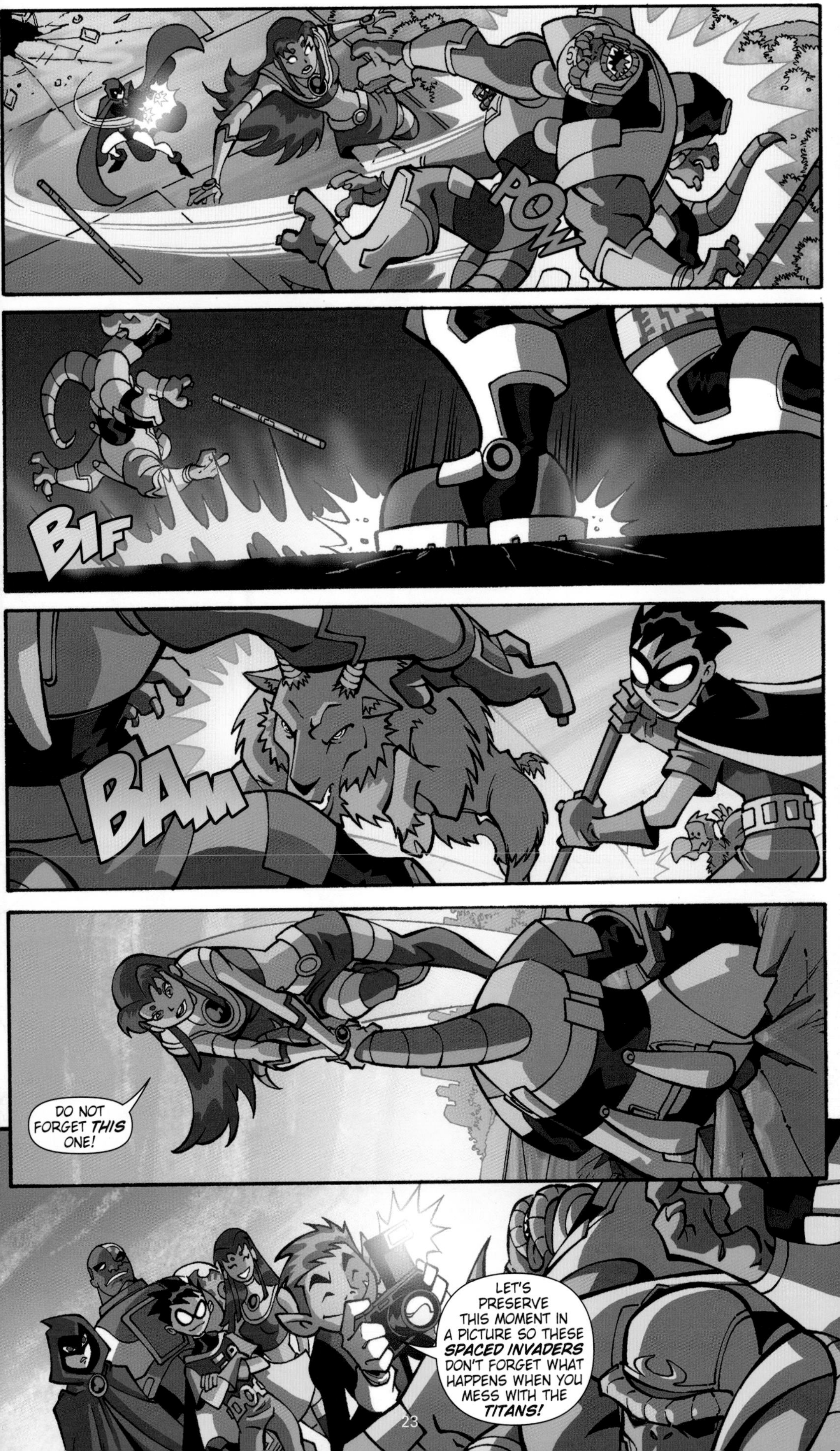
POW
BIF
BAM
DO NOT FORGET THIS ONE!
LET'S PRESERVE THIS MOMENT IN A PICTURE SO THESE SPACED INVADERS DON'T FORGET WHAT HAPPENS WHEN YOU MESS WITH THE TITANS!

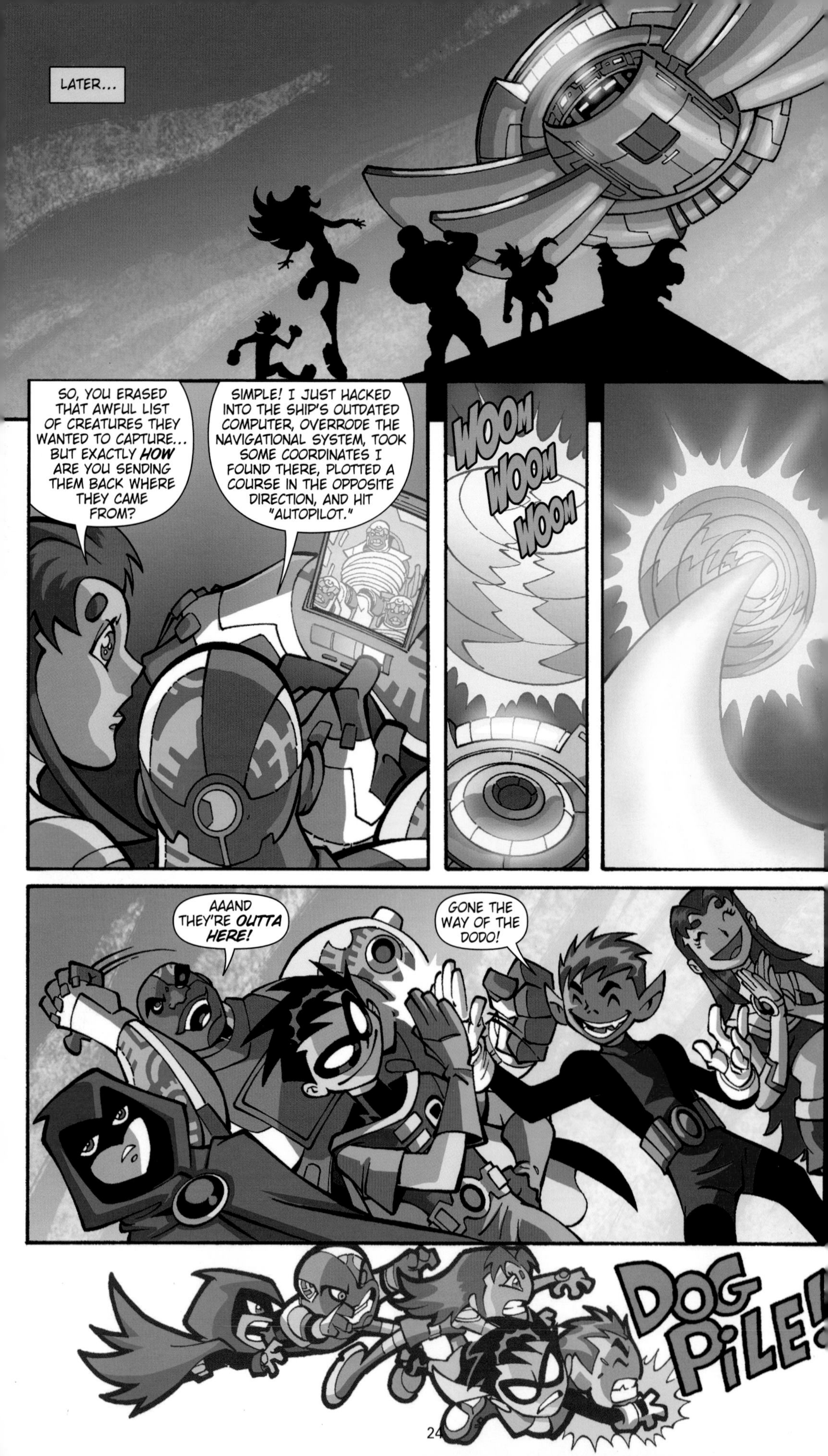
LATER...
SO, YOU ERASED THAT AWFUL LIST OF CREATURES THEY WANTED TO CAPTURE... BUT EXACTLY HOW ARE YOU SENDING THEM BACK WHERE THEY CAME FROM?
SIMPLE! I JUST HACKED INTO THE SHIP'S OUTDATED COMPUTER, OVERRODE THE NAVIGATIONAL SYSTEM, TOOK SOME COORDINATES I FOUND THERE, PLOTTED A COURSE IN THE OPPOSITE DIRECTION, AND HIT "AUTOPILOT."
WOOM WOOM WOOM
AAAND THEY'RE OUTTA HERE!
GONE THE WAY OF THE DODO!
DOG PILE!

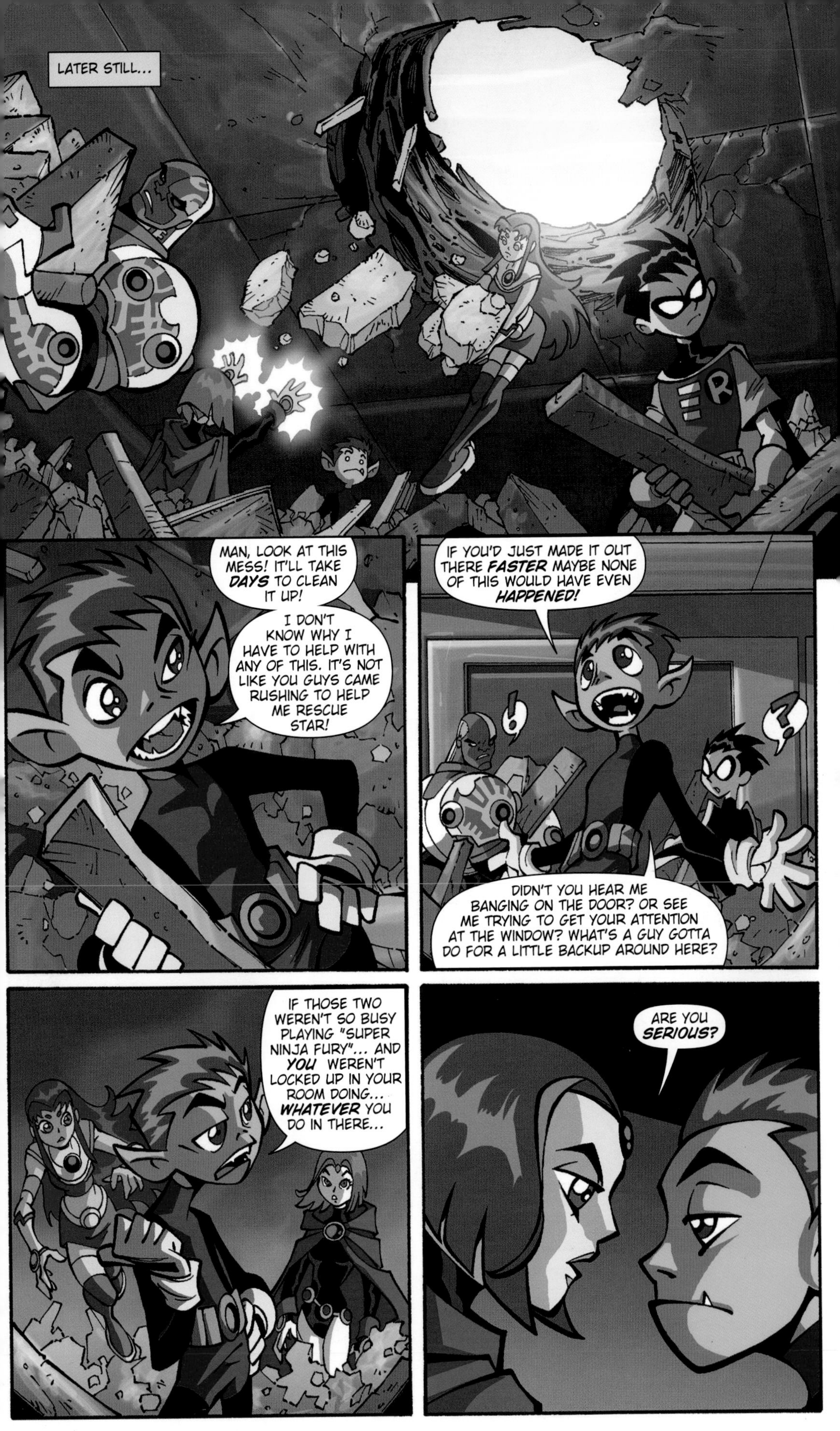
LATER STILL...
MAN, LOOK AT THIS MESS! IT'LL TAKE DAYS TO CLEAN IT UP!
I DON'T KNOW WHY I HAVE TO HELP WITH ANY OF THIS. IT'S NOT LIKE YOU GUYS CAME RUSHING TO HELP ME RESCUE STAR!
IF YOU'D JUST MADE IT OUT THERE FASTER MAYBE NONE OF THIS WOULD HAVE EVEN HAPPENED!
DIDN'T YOU HEAR ME BANGING ON THE DOOR? OR SEE ME TRYING TO GET YOUR ATTENTION AT THE WINDOW? WHAT'S A GUY GOTTA DO FOR A LITTLE BACKUP AROUND HERE?
IF THOSE TWO WEREN'T SO BUSY PLAYING "SUPER NINJA FURY"... AND YOU WEREN'T LOCKED UP IN YOUR ROOM DOING... WHATEVER YOU DO IN THERE...
ARE YOU SERIOUS?

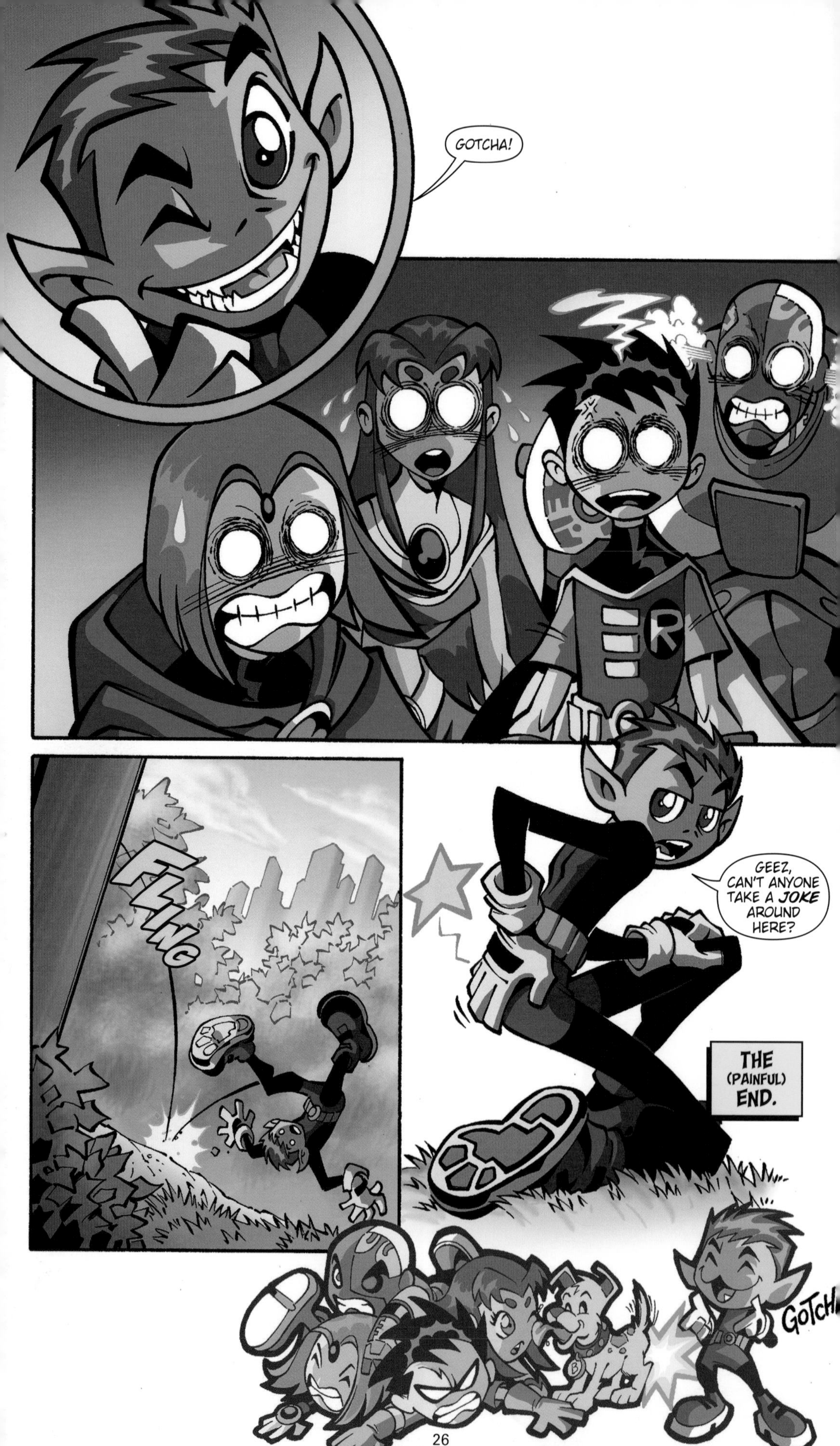
GOTCHA!
FLING
GEEZ, CAN'T ANYONE TAKE A JOKE AROUND HERE?
THE (PAINFUL) END.
GOTCH

# CREATORS

## J. TORRES WRITER

J. Torres won the Shuster Award for Outstanding Writer for his work on Batman: Legends of the Dark Knight, Love As a Foreign Language, and Teen Titans Go! He is also the writer of the Eisner Award nominated Alison Dare and the YALSA listed Days Like This and Lola: A Ghost Story. Other comic book credits include Avatar: The Last Airbender, Batman: The Brave and the Bold, Legion of Super-Heroes in the 31st Century, Ninja Scroll, Wonder Girl, Wonder Woman, and WALL-E: Recharge.

## TODD NAUCK ARTIST

Todd Nauck is an American comic book artist and writer. Nauck is most notable for his work on Young Justice, Teen Titans Go!, and his own creation, Wildguard.

# GLOSSARY

*captivity* (KAP-tiv-i-tee)--that state of being imprisoned, confined, or enslaved

*database* (DAY-tuh-bayss)--the information that is organized and stored in a computer

*detain* (di-TAYN)--to hold somebody back when they want to go or leave

*dodo* (DOH-doh)--a clumsy, flightless, extinct bird

*expires* (ek-SPY-urs)--dies or ends

*extinct* (ek-STINGKT)--died out, or no longer in existence

*habitat* (HAB-uh-tat)--natural environment

*ingenious* (in-JEE-nee-uhss)--clever or creative

*intruder* (in-TROO-dur)--someone who enters an area without permission

*invaders* (in-VAY-durz)--people who enter forcefully as enemies

*overrode* (oh-vur-RODE)--overruled, or had final say over something

# VISUAL QUESTIONS & PROMPTS

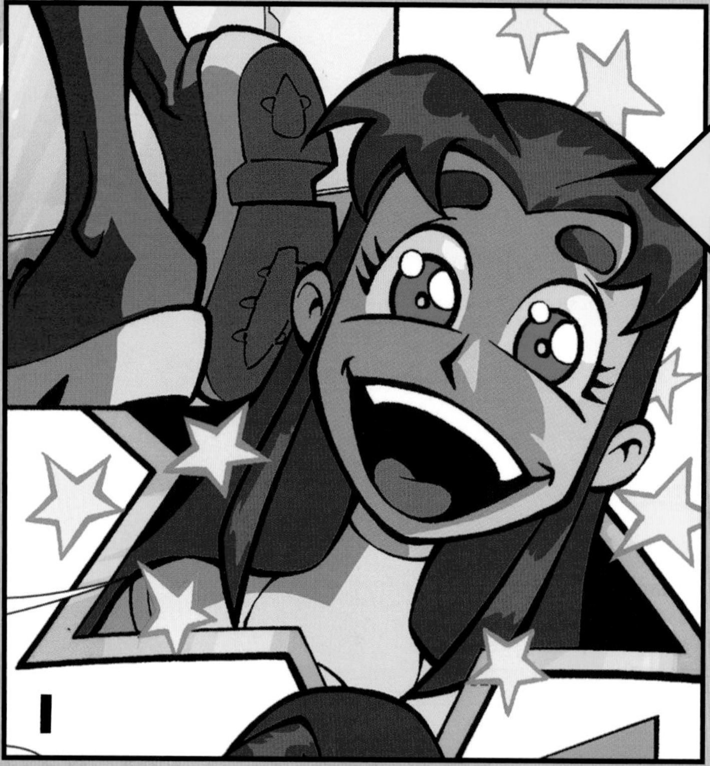

1. On page 9, Starfire is seen with stars circling her head. Based on the surrounding pages, what do you think the stars mean? How does she feel, and why?

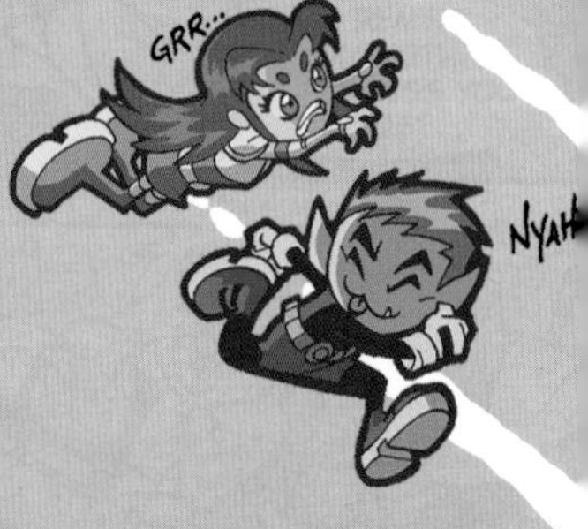
GRR...
NYAH

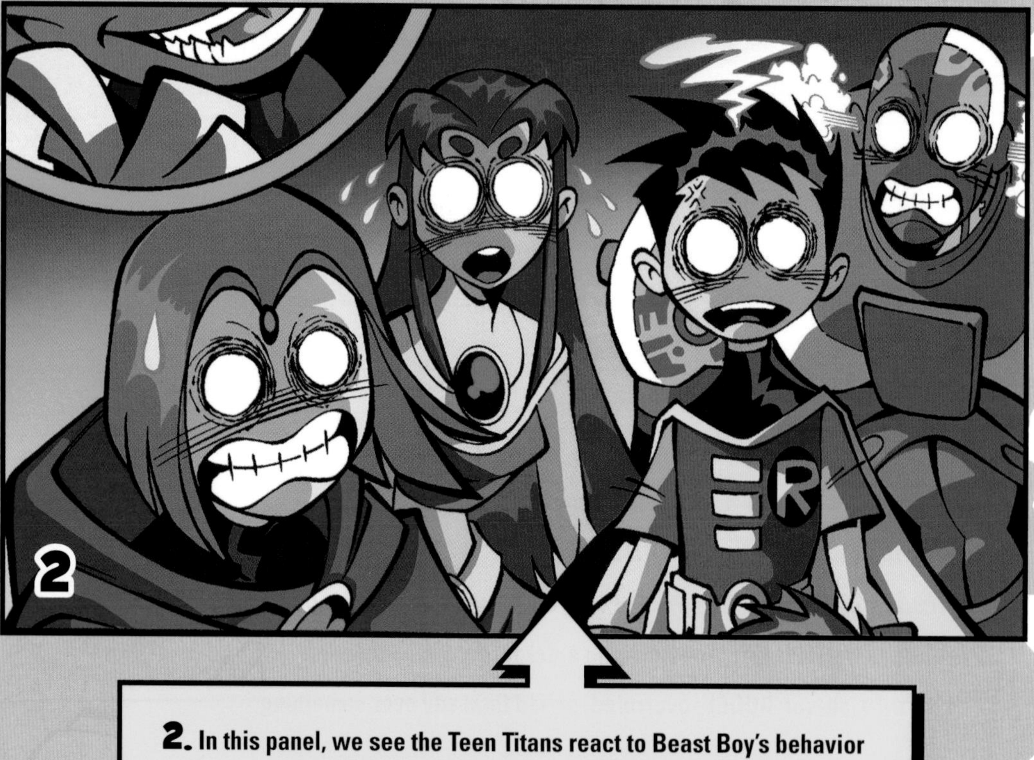

2. In this panel, we see the Teen Titans react to Beast Boy's behavior on page 26. Why did they react the way they did in this panel?

**3.** In these two panels, we see Beast Boy being thrown from the Teen Titans base. Who threw him out, and why? Reread pages 25-26 if you aren't sure.

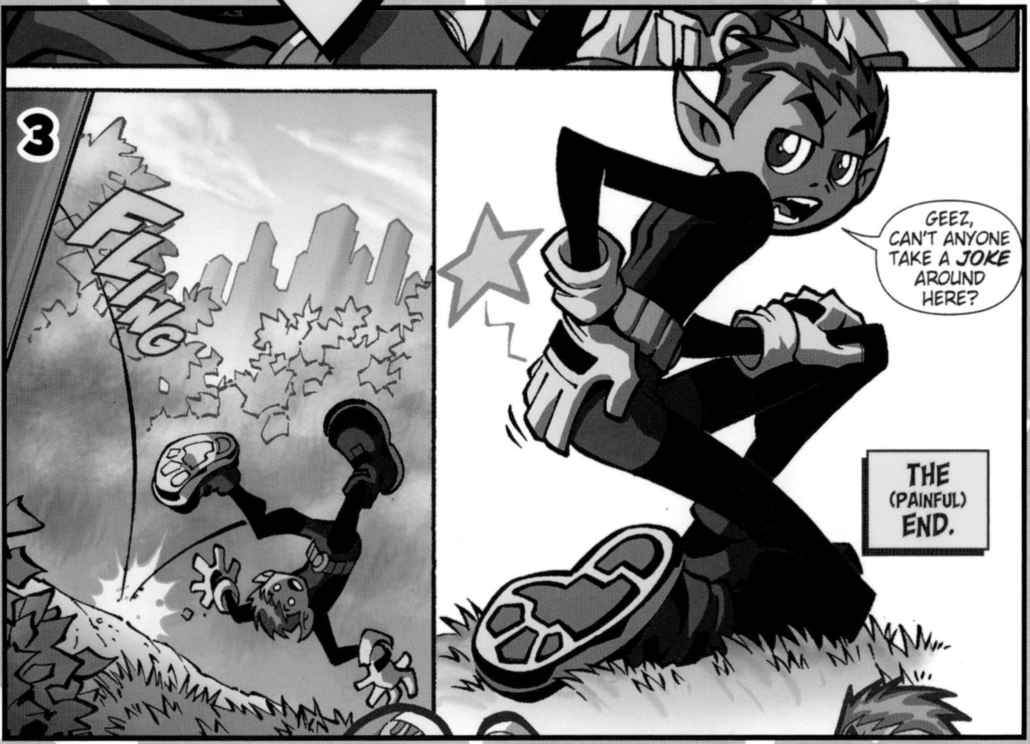
3
FLING
GEEZ, CAN'T ANYONE TAKE A *JOKE* AROUND HERE?
THE (PAINFUL) END.

**4.** To "cry wolf" means to raise a false alarm. How did Beast Boy cry wolf in this book? How did it end up hurting him? Explain your answers.

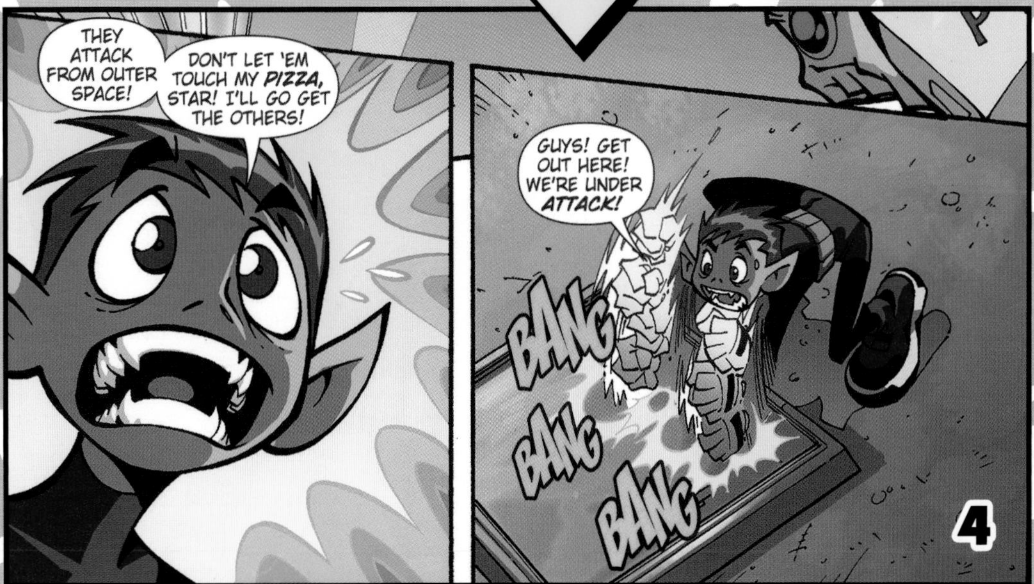
THEY ATTACK FROM OUTER SPACE!
DON'T LET 'EM TOUCH MY *PIZZA*, STAR! I'LL GO GET THE OTHERS!
GUYS! GET OUT HERE! WE'RE UNDER *ATTACK!*
BANG
BANG
BANG
4

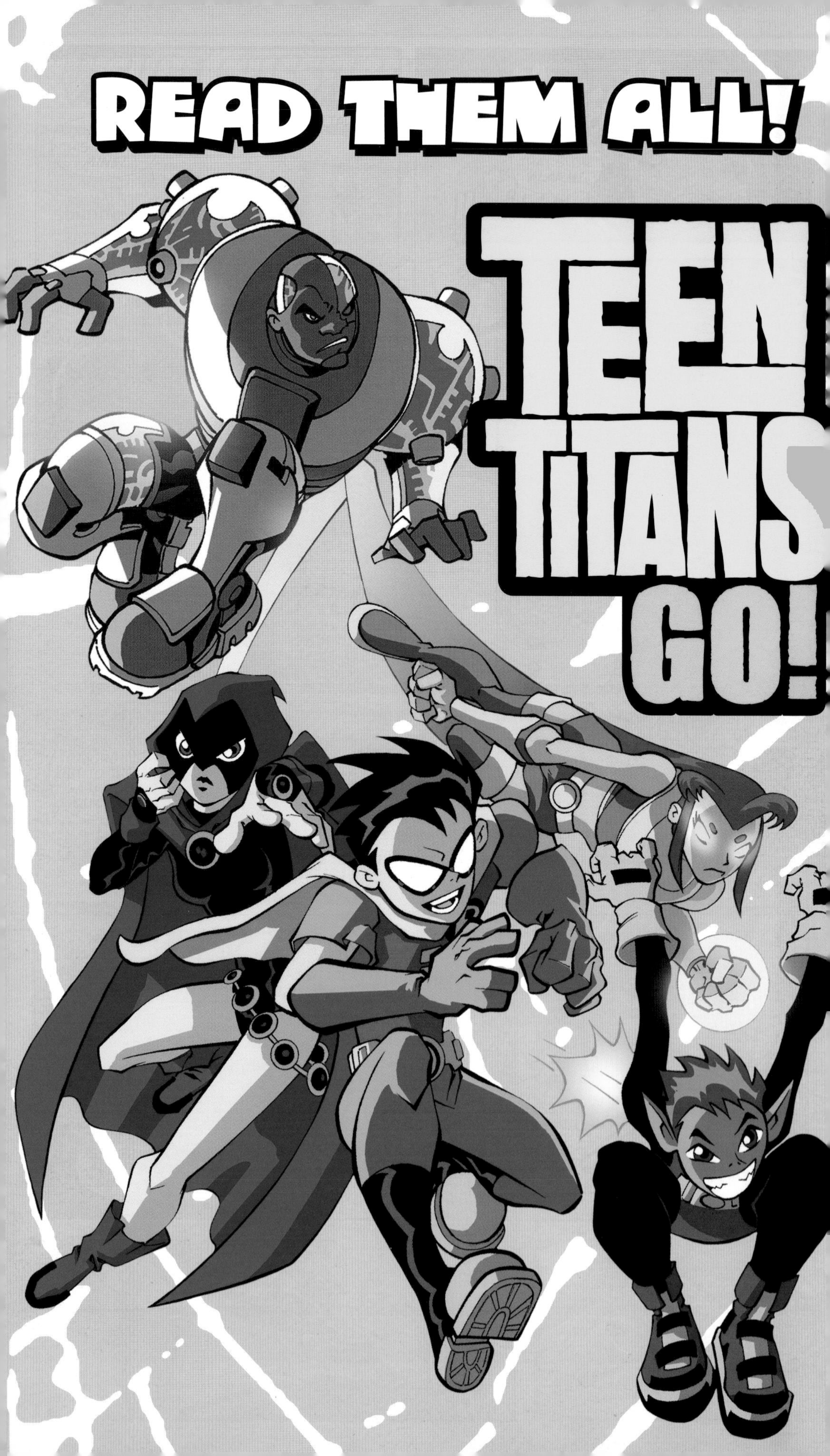
READ THEM ALL!
TEEN TITANS GO!

TEEN TITANS GO!®

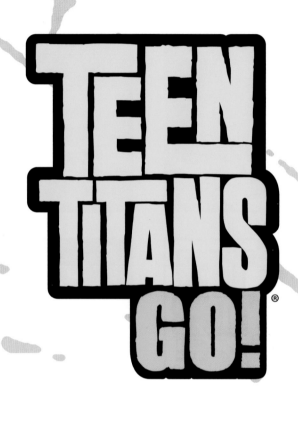